CASTLE VALLEY

CASTLE VALLEY

THE ADVENTURES OF DAL TRENT

T. ROSS CHASE

XULON PRESS

Xulon Press
2301 Lucien Way #415
Maitland, FL 32751
407.339.4217
www.xulonpress.com

Paperback ISBN-13: 978-1-66284-557-4
Ebook ISBN-13: 978-1-66284558-1

Dedication

I would like to take this opportunity to acknowledge and thank everyone who has helped me as I wrote this book. My wife, Mary, has encouraged me more than once to keep on going! I started writing this many years ago, and she would ask me, "have you done any more on your book?" She was my inspiration for coming back time and again to write just a little more!! Thank you, Honey!! I love you!

My three daughters were also involved with getting me to write a little more. Thank you, Andrea, Kathryn, and Deborah. I love you guys too!!

A special thank you is due to my good friend and sister-in-Christ, Beverly May. She took my draft and put it together. There's a story here! Because I started this project many years ago, the computer I used then had a different format than the ones now. So everything that was written on that old computer, was all jumbled up. Punctuation, spacing, everything!! Bev took it and worked her magic for me. Bev, thank you from the bottom of my heart!!

Another person who, I feel is responsible for me to even attempt to write is my English teacher in high school. Her name was Ann Brown. She always would tell me, "you need to write." She would tell me to "be more descriptive!" Mrs. Brown, I don't know where you are, but if you by any chance read this, thank you for your encouragement.

Finally, and most of all, I would like to thank my Lord and Savior, Jesus Christ, for His love and forgiveness that assure me of a home in Heaven!

About the Author

Born and raised in a small rural town, T. Ross Chase has lived a quiet life amid the White Mountains of New Hampshire. With no desire to live anywhere else, he still has had a keen interest in the American West, especially The High Lonesome, where the mountain man resided.

When asked about his favorite author, he will tell you it is Louis Lamour. He has read every book he could get his hands on that Mr. Lamour wrote about life in those Western mountains. "I could always picture myself walking in the boots of those characters that Mr. Lamour wrote about. I was right there through the whole book. I can only hope that I might hold your attention through my writings, the same as Mr. Lamour does in his."

Foreword

Dal Trent is one of those men who you would much rather be his friend than his enemy! Hardened from life in the High Lonesome, he faced any problem head on. Our story finds him in a tough situation even for him, as he is faced with survival in a full blown blizzard with no shelter or wood for a fire. He knows from experience that if he doesn't find shelter, and fast, he might not make it to the morning! Come alongside Dal, and experience with him, the beauty of the Rocky Mountains, and the hardships associated with living his life there!

Introduction

The snow continued to fall heavily, with flakes as big as silver dollars, straight to the ground. The wind was still, and the silence was so complete it was unnerving. Two feet of fresh powder already blanketed the slope without any signs of stopping. Wildlife was instinctively holed up waiting out the storm. The only movement was that of a solitary figure, huddled against the falling snow. The man had his own instinct, and it was telling him he must find shelter soon, but shelter was hard to come by on this side of the mountain. If something didn't present itself soon, he would be forced to spend another cold night in the open. He wasn't sure if he could survive another night without the warmth of a fire. The temperature was sure to drop with the oncoming darkness, and more than likely, the wind would start up again, driving the cold still deeper into his bones.

It wasn't his first time caught in a situation of this sort, but it never got any easier. This was his third winter in the Central Rockies, and he understood that if he chose to stay here, he would probably not live to see his thirtieth birthday. Not that he ever really kept track of birthdays, but he had a rough idea of when it was each year. As near as he could cipher, he was twentysix only last month. December was now in its third week, and the days were so short he often found himself falling short of his main camp, having checked the trapline that he laid out in early September. Back then, with more hours of sunlight, it was not difficult at all for him to check the traps and be back at camp with time to spare before darkness settled over the area. It was the hardest work he had ever done, but it was proving to be a very worthwhile business. Prime furs, back in the settlements, were as good as gold, and if things continued as they had so far, he would be a rich man come spring. Not that money really mattered to him. What would he spend it on anyway? With the nearest settlement miles away, it hardly did any good to have money. He only made three, maybe four trips into town a year. Once in the spring to replenish his depleted supplies, once or twice during the summer just to keep him up to date on what was happening, and once in the fall to stock up for the long winter months ahead.

His name was Dal Trent, and he was originally from East of the great river. It was generally believed, by those who were acquainted with him, that he hailed from Tennessee. He never really talked much about his past, and not too many dared ask. Men of his caliber, and from this particular time in history, always seemed to be surrounded with yarns. How many were true and how many were made up around lonely campfires, well, you just didn't ask! Just the fact that he had lived in the wilderness alone, and survived, for these past three years spoke volumes about the man, and anyone familiar with the hardships suffered, knew that no ordinary man could survive. And so it was, that since he was no ordinary man, he was looked upon as a six-foot, seven-inch legend.

The legend, now stood in snow almost up to his knees, and knew he was in trouble. The wind had begun to pick up and was now whipping snow into his face, stinging his eyes and sticking to his beard. What he needed right now was a small miracle. He needed shelter. A place he could start a fire and get out of the wind. He always carried jerked meat with him so he knew he wasn't in danger of starving, but being caught out in the open, at night was almost sure to get him frozen to death by morning.

Visibility was not any better than it had been earlier, and it was difficult to see more than fifty feet in any direction. He wasn't even sure he was going in the right direction anymore, what with the blowing snow and all. He was just going to have to trust in his instincts to pull him out of this one. Of course, a little prayer now and then doesn't hurt either! You don't live in the High

Lonesome for very long and doubt that there is a God that put all of this together.

And so it was that the legend knelt in the mounting snow and asked the Creator to see him through one more night. It was not something he was ashamed to do, and he would have done the same thing had he been surrounded by his peers. It always seemed natural to be on speaking terms with the One who had made all of this beauty, and it sure didn't hurt in times like this.

"Dal Trent, you're a durned fool, getting yourself in this predicament," he said out loud to himself. "If the Almighty doesn't see fit to save your old carcass, you'll be frizzed harder'n a rock come mornin'."

Sometimes talking to oneself helped to fill the void of not having anyone around to carry on a conversation with. Of course, you had to be careful of where you talked to yourself. You never talked to yourself out loud when there was danger of Indians being in hearing distance, if you wanted to keep your hair, or if you were in close proximity of a grizzly, if you wanted to keep anything!

Dal knew that right now there was no danger of either Injun or bear being out in this storm. He was the only one fool enough to be out for a stroll today.

Suddenly, he thought he saw the outline of trees ahead. He couldn't be sure because of the blowing and swirling snow, but for an instant he was positive he saw trees. Continuing on in that direction, he eventually came to a small group of conifers. Nothing that would offer a great deal of protection, but it certainly was better than having none at all!

Near the center of the group of trees, he scooped out the snow down to the ground, and taking from his pack a small amount of dried moss, carried for just such an emergency, and his flint and steel, he broke off some of the dried lower branches from the trees nearest to him, and built a small fire, adding more wood as the fire grew in size. In just a short time, he had a fire large enough to provide the much- needed warmth. The trees provided the shelter from the wind so the fire wouldn't blow out, and by digging a hole in the snow next to the fire, he could stay relatively warm.

He gathered enough wood to take him through the night, and then settled down in his little nest to enjoy the heat and a piece of venison jerky. As he sat there and pondered his situation, he realized that it hadn't been long after he had resorted to a whispered prayer, that the shelter had come into sight. He made a mental note to remember this and someday he would think on it more in depth. Right now, he needed sleep, and it wasn't long before he was snoring. Morning might present more problems for him, but right now he was warm, his belly was reasonably full, and he was getting rest.

Chapter One

Dalton Eugene Trent was born fourth, in a family of eight, at a time when every family was selfsufficient. You were either selfsufficient or you starved. And with a large family, and even more mouths to feed, times seemed even more harsh. However, though there were days when they didn't know if there would be food on the table, there was a closeness of being together that helped them pull through.

Dal s father, Warren, was by trade, a carpenter. They had moved to the Ohio River Valley in the year 1798. The Indian wars were ended in 1795 and Warren was convinced this was the break he had been searching for. He had always loved the sense of accomplishment at looking at something he had made with his own two hands, and he always strived to search for ways to improve his skills. This move would allow him to expand his abilities, as well as helping the country on its Westward advance. There would be many who would be needing help in building cabins and furnishings. While there probably wouldn't be much money for

his services, people always were willing to swap whatever they had, such as milk, eggs, vegetables, meat, etc.

The land was rich and would provide for their sustenance. All they had to do was till the soil and plant
the seeds. This job seemed to fall on Dal, since he
was the oldest boy. His two older sisters, Hannah, and
Rebecca, helped when they could, but their time was
mostly spent helping their mother who always seemed
to have a new baby in her arms.

By the time Dal was sixteen years old, he was able
to carry his end of the work that was expected of him,
and he was even helping his father build cabins. His
father always seemed to take it for granted that Dal
would follow in his footsteps as a carpenter. Dal had
other ideas but continued to keep them to himself. In
those days you didn't voice your opinions too much if
you were only a boy, unless you were asked. And Dal
wasn't asked, at least by his father. His mother, Mary,
often engaged Dal in conversation when Warren was
off on a job, and so she knew that Dal would not pursue
carpentry as a trade. She would often see the dreamy
look in his eyes when they talked of the unsettled land
to the West of them, so she suspected that when he was
old enough, that would be the direction he would take.

Mary didn't disclose to Warren the talks she had
with her son, because she knew that he wouldn't
approve. She knew that when the time came, there

would be plenty of discussion. She also knew that any amount of discussion would not change Dal's already made-up mind. She would certainly hate to see him leave, being her oldest boy and all, but she wouldn't stand in his way. She'd even help to change Warren's mind if needed. He had followed his dream when he had moved them to the Ohio River Valley, and no one had tried to stop him, not that it would have done any good anyway. She could see Warren in Dal more every day. She knew this was a good thing because Warren was a man you could count on. He was a man of his word, and if he shook hands on anything, that was the same as being written in stone. He was well known and respected for miles around even though they had only been here for a little under a year. He stood for what was right. He had been a strong influence on Dal.

She remembered the day, only a month ago, when Dal had to go about a mile and a half to help his dad on a new house. They had to erect some large timbers and Warren couldn't manage alone. After Dal had finished with his morning chores, which consisted of milking the cows, putting them out to pasture, gathering the eggs, feeding the hens, and working in the garden, he was supposed to walk to his father's jobsite. He had left about midmorning and Mary didn't expect to see him again until evening. Much to her surprise, he had returned, with his father just before lunchtime. Dal s face was swollen and bloody and his clothes were torn and covered with mud. She could tell from the look on Warren s face that he was outraged.

"Dal, what happened to you? Are you O.K.?" asked Mary.

"If you can get him to tell you what he's been up to, you're doin' better'n me," barked Warren. "He won't tell me a thing of what happened! It's obvious he's been fightin', and if he don't tell us about it, he's headed for the woodshed! See if he'll talk to you. I'm goin' outside for a spell."

Mary got some hot water from the stove and some bandages and proceeded to clean her boy up. Dal winced as she wiped the caked-on blood and dirt from his bruised face.

"Are you going to tell me what happened?" Mary asked him. "Have you been fighting?"

"Yeah, I've been fightin', but it had to be," Dal answered in a matter-of-fact voice.

"Tell me about it, Dal," said his mother almost in a whisper as she dabbed at his face.

"There's nothin' ta tell, Ma. I got in a fight is all. I know I 'done wrong and I'm willin' ta take the consequences for it."

Warren came into the room and stood there glowering at Dal. "Well, did he say what he was fightin' for?"

"He won't say, Warren. Can't you just let it slide this once? I'm sure he must have had a good reason for what he did," pleaded Mary.

"I can't, Mary. If I do, he'll just do it again." Turning to Dal, he said, "go to the woodshed and wait for me there, boy."

Dal slowly got to his feet and stood eye to eye with his father. "You're right, pa. I would do the same thing again. He turned on his heal and walked out the door."

Warren looked at Mary and saw the pleading in her eyes, but he knew he had to follow through. He had always had a rule about fighting, and Dal had known it. He would just have to suffer the consequences.

He knew that Dal was as strong as he himself was, and he half expected Dal to challenge him. As he rounded the corner to the woodshed, he saw Dal sitting on the chopping block, waiting for him. His head was resting in his hands, and Warren was reminded of the times he had done this before. He had to steel himself if he was going to get through this.

"Stand up and turn around Dal," he said as he pulled off his belt. Dal stood and turned around without saying a word. The sound of the belt cut the air as it descended onto the backside of Warren's son, and tears filled the father's eyes as he thought of the pain he was inflicting. He hit him three times and could not bring himself to do it the fourth. Warren slid his belt back in his pants, and Dal turned around to face his father. Not a sign of a tear was in his eyes, and it was at this moment that Warren knew he would never raise his hand again to his boy. Dal was a man, and what he hadn't already learned, he probably never would. Warren knew he had done his best in bringing his children up to know right from wrong, and he had done a pretty good job of it.

Dal left the woodshed without saying a word to his father and walked out past the barn where the two cows were grazing contentedly, and the chickens were scratching in the barnyard. He walked straight past where he had helped pull stumps to make way for a cornfield and into the woods. This was where he always felt at ease. He could be himself here. How many days he had spent here as a boy dreaming of the day when he would be on his own, free to pursue his dream of going west. He had even practiced moving about the woods in a manner that would make him blend with his surroundings. He had gotten pretty good at it too. He recalled the time he had sneaked up on his two older sisters, when they had been out picking berries. They hadn't heard or seen him as he approached within ten feet of them. He had then lain there and listened to their talk of boys.

Hannah had told Rebecca that she had taken a shine to that boy that lived over across the creek. His name was Henry Tibbets and she had told how she had met him down by the swimming hole one day. He had stolen a kiss and then run away. She had sworn Rebecca to silence. Dal had all he could do to contain himself and keep from bursting out laughing. The girls had drifted toward the house, picking berries as they went, and he had remained hidden until they were out of sight.

That night, while sitting around the table eating supper, Dal had casually mentioned having seen Henry Tibbets and then he had winked at Hannah. Her face had turned a dozen shades of red, and she gave Rebecca a withering look and a kick under the table. To this day, Hannah still thought that Rebecca had told Dal about the kiss!

Yes, he could think better in the woods. He was in his element here. He was home. He would be heading west one of these days. He had saved enough money to buy that rifle old man Jenkins had shown him. And what a deal it was! It fit his hands like it was made for him. The balance was just right, and he had even been allowed to shoot it once! Mr. Jenkins knew how much Dal wanted this gun, and he had told him he would keep it just for him.

Tomorrow, Dal would make a visit to Mr. Jenkins and that gun would be his. Then all he had to do was wait till the time was right, and he would be on his way West!!

Chapter Two

He wondered how pa was going to react when he showed him the rifle. He knew he didn't have any objections to guns, because out here a gun was an essential part of life. It could mean the difference between life or death. It was the part about spending his money on it that Dal thought he would object to. Money was not something easily acquired.

Dal walked into the yard, with his new rifle under his arm, and a good-sized deer slung over his shoulder. He didn't figure it would hurt to have a peace offering along just in case things didn't go well. It was a warm spring evening and ma and pa were sitting on the porch reading to the younger children. They all looked up when they heard someone approaching, and the children, when they saw it was him, came bounding off the steps and almost knocked Dal over in their exuberance.

Warren came off the porch and took the deer from off Dal s shoulder. "Nice deer, where'd you happen on him?"

"Down by the edge of the cornfield. He was headed down to the creek for a drink. I guess I kind of deprived him of that!" Dal said with a twinkle in his eye.

"Where did you get the gun, that looks like a beauty," Warren said.

"Mr. Jenkins saved it for me. He's had it for about six months, and when he knew I wanted it, he said he would keep it for me, and when I had the money, I could buy it. It fits me just like it was made for me, and it shoots like a dream. Would you like to shoot it pa"?

"No thanks, son. You'll probably need all the ammunition you can get when you get out to the Rocky Mountains!" Dal was stunned and couldn't think of what to say for a minute." He looked at his mother and she just shrugged her shoulders as much as to say, I don t know anything about this!

"How did you know, pa?" Dal asked.

"A father has a way of knowing things. I've suspected for some time that you had a desire to go awondering. I was just biding my time, to see what would happen. I knew it was only a matter of time. I just want you to know that you have our blessing. Don t forget what we have tried to teach you these past years. And if you ever want to come home, do it. We'll be here."

"Thanks pa," Dal said blinking back tears. "It means a lot to me to have yours and ma's blessing."

"Oh, and one more thing, Dal," pa said. "I was talking with the blacksmith in town today, and he was telling me of an incident that happened the other day, along the road that leads to that house I was building.

He said that a new girl to the neighborhood had been walking along the road that led into town, when she was accosted by three boys. Seems like they tried to have their way with her but were stopped by a boy she didn't recognize. Have you any idea who that boy might've been, Dal?" Dal stood there kicking at the dirt with the toe of his boot and acting like he wished he were somewhere else. "Well, boy?"

"I reckon that was me, pa."

"Why didn't you tell me that was what happened? I never would have taken the belt to you, had I known."

"Well, pa, I'd been fightin, and you had a rule about fightin. I didn't think it mattered what the reason was."

"Son, if you're in the right and you know your right, then sometimes there just ain't no way around it. Just make sure, beyond a doubt, that you're right."

"Do you think I'm right in wanting to head West, Pa?"

"Only you know the answer to that, son. Sometimes there's only one way to find out. And that is to do it."

"Well, Pa, I reckon I aim to do just that. The summer is drawing to a close, and if you and Ma can get along without me, I'd better get started. Snow comes early in them mountains, and I'd like to get some shelter built and some food stored up."

"We'll hate to see you go, Dal. You'll be hard to replace around here, even though we have plenty of us left. I reckon we can spare some corn and jerked meat,

10

and I bet your Ma can cook you up some biscuits and cornbread. That should last you till you get to them mountains at least. And there's one more thing I'd like you to take with you. Come with me." Dal followed his father into the back room where most of their stuff was stored that wasn't used very often. For the most part, this room had been off limits to the children, so Dal had no idea what to expect. Warren opened a wooden chest, and Dal could see various types of woodworking tools in it. Reaching down, Warren pulled out a tanned leather pouch tied with a leather thong. He handed it to Dal and told him to open it. Dal took the pouch and laid it on the bench. He looked over at his father and he nodded for Dal to open it.

Dal slowly untied the thong and folded back the top of the pouch. From within came a glint of steel unlike Dal had ever seen. He pulled out a knife that was all of eighteen inches long. The blade was at least a foot long with a keen edge and sharp point. It had been polished until it shone. The handle was made from bone and had been engraved with hunting scenes.

Dal turned to face his dad. Their eyes locked for a few seconds and then they threw their arms around each other in a fierce bear hug. Tears fell from both pair of eyes as they cherished this father, son moment.

Dal was the first to speak. "Where did you ever get such a beautiful knife?"

"Well as you know, some of the people I work for can't pay with money, so they give me what they have. Sometime ago now, I built a cabin and all the furnishings for an old man and his wife down where the river turns and heads away from town. You know the cabin that sets right on the point there?"

"Yeah, I know the one. His son went west didn't he? Seems like his name was Eban. Didn't something happen to him?"

"He was found dead next to one of the trails. Luckily, he was found by someone who was honest. They sent his belongings back to his parents. This knife was his. His parents never knew where he had gotten it, and they gave it to me in payment for their house. I really didn't know what I would ever do with it, but that was about all they had, so I took it. I hope It serves you well, and I'm glad I can give it to you."

"I could only have dreamed about owning something as beautiful as this. Thanks, Pa."

"You're welcome, son. Now I think you have some packing to do before night falls. When do you plan on leaving?'

"I think I'll leave at first light. I'm anxious to get started. I'll say goodbye to all of you tonight, and I won't have to wake you in the morning."

"Well, if that's the case, I'll help you get your things together. The rest of the family is going to want to spend as much time with you tonight as possible. It may be quite a spell before we see you again."

Chapter Three

Somewhere in the night, a wolf howled, answered by another and another. Dal stirred and then drifted back to sleep. Again, only closer this time, the wolves broke the silence with that unnerving sound. The sound that made the hairs on the back of your neck stand on end. The sound that seemed to penetrate your very being. Dal was awake this time and reached out to add more wood to the dying embers of his campfire. The wood cracked, and finally caught, sending a new light into the intense blackness that surrounded him. The flames licked higher, and he added a few more larger pieces assuring that the fire would last. The warmth from the fire felt good to his tired and aching body. How far he had come and had yet to go to reach his shelter, he wasn't sure. The falling snow had made it impossible to recognize any landmarks. He noticed now that the snow had all but stopped. That at least was good, but with the stopping of the snow, the temperature usually dropped considerably. He had seen it drop as much as forty degrees in a short time. This could be dangerous if he wasn't careful. He would have to take care that he didn't work up a sweat while he was wading through the snow. That sweat could turn to ice against his skin and mean the death of him. He'd have to take It slow and easy. Sometimes that was a hard thing for him to do because he was one to walk at a pretty good pace. Most men would have been hard put to keep up with him at just his normal walk. When he really wanted to cover some ground, most men would have been left far behind. He'd just have to take it easy.

He settled back into his little hole in the snow and let the warmth of the fire wash over him. Tomorrow, if he was lucky, he would make it back to his shelter, where he had plenty of food and wood. He could hole up there as long as he needed to. If there was one thing he had learned in this country, it was that when you thought you had enough supplies to last you the winter, you'd better put by as much again. It had saved his life more than once.

His eyes grew heavy once more and soon he was fast asleep. The wolves had come as close to the fire as they dared. They could smell the man and the meat he carried in his sack. It had been a long time since they had eaten. The deep snow was making it increasingly difficult to find food. Here, at last, they had found food, but they were instinctively afraid of the fire. They continued to keep their distance as the flames danced in the night and made weird shapes against the trees.

Unless a hand continues to feed an open fire, its fuel is devoured in a short time. Such was the case now. The flames gradually died down to embers, and only gave off a small glow as it continued to die. The wolves were bolder now that the fire was almost out. The smell of meat was in their noses and their stomachs growled in anticipation of food. Three shadows in the night crept forward, closer, and closer to their intended meal. The man smell was strong, but their need to eat was stronger. They were close enough to be able to tell from where the smell of meat was coming from. It was in the sack that this man had his head on. One wolf had his head within inches of the man's face when an arrow came out of nowhere and buried itself in the side of the wolf. It yelped and sank to the ground, causing the other two to turn tail and run. Dal came to with a start and grabbed his rifle. He stayed low in his nest and waited. He could see the wolf that only lay a few feet away with the arrow sticking out and knew he was not alone. But should he be afraid? Whoever was out there, could just as easily have shot him with an arrow instead of the wolf. Or they could have let the wolf have him. But he knew that Indians were beyond understanding. They might only have saved his life so they could torture him later.

If he only knew how many there were. He certainly couldn't watch all sides at once, and if they could shoot

16

the wolf that easily, certainly he could be next. He studied the wolf carcass and decided that the arrow had come from the direction he himself had come before bedding down. He kept watch for the slightest movement in that direction but saw none. His senses were all alert now and his nose moved like a hound on the scent, as his eyes darted here and there. His ears were tuned for even the slightest sound.

Someone must have come across his tracks and followed him here. They must have been close because the snow had been falling so fast that his tracks would have been obliterated in a matter of minutes.

He continued to lay dead still, not daring the slightest move. After what seemed an eternity, but in reality, only a few minutes, he began to relax. He felt rather sure that if whoever was out there had meant him any harm, he would either be dead or a prisoner by now. He knew that dawn was not far away, and he had only a little time to wait before the sun would be up. He checked his powder to make sure it was dry and loosened the knife his father had given him in its sheath. His hatchet was in his belt and ready for when and if he needed it. He had one pistol and he checked to make sure it was loaded and primed. Now all he had to do was wait for morning.

The first light seemed slow in coming, but soon the whole sky was painted with the rays of the sun as it poked its head over the eastern horizon. The snow glittered like so many diamonds and seemed to give off a pinkish glow. Dal used this time to study his surroundings. There were many things he had not seen last night on his way in during the snowstorm. For instance, there was a small stream off to his left that ran parallel to the thicket he had spent the night in. He could make out the stream as it wound down the valley and it seemed to end on what looked like a meadow. This must be a beaver dam. If it was, it was the largest one Dal had ever seen. It must have encompassed at least four or five acres. He would have to remember its location. There would be a good number of beavers to be had for the taking, along with muskrat and otter.

The valley continued to fall away below him, and it seemed he could see for miles. It ran SouthSoutheast which explained why the sun had reached him sooner than usual. He studied both sides of the valley for landmarks that might give him a hint of where he was. Off to his right, the mountains ran up steeply, and though they were at least a mile or more away, they were awe inspiring. He never ceased to marvel at these mountains, and the land he now called his home. As he scanned the lesser mountains and hills on his left, he caught sight of an outcropping of rock that he was sure was the one called Tomahawk Ridge. It was given its name, as legend had it, not only because it resembled

18

a crude tomahawk, but also the local Indians used to get the rocks used in making the heads of their tomahawks there. If this was indeed Tomahawk Ridge he had sighted, his shelter wasn't more than an hour from it. If all went well, he should be home by high noon.

First, he had to determine where his night visitor had come from, and where he had gone. He walked to the dead wolf and stooped down and pulled the arrow out. He turned it over and over in his hand. The feathers and markings on the shaft were that of the Cheyenne tribe. He walked to where he could see tracks in the snow and found where someone had crouched in the snow. It appeared he had been there for quite some time, for the area was well packed. The footprint was very small, and it seemed to be the only one there. Probably this was a young buck on a manhood trial. But it nagged at the back of Dals' mind that he could just as easily have been the one with the arrow sticking out of his ribcage. He wasn't sure the wolf would have attacked him, but he certainly had gotten close. Too close! Whoever this was just may have saved his life. But why? Had this young buck brought back his scalp, wouldn't that have meant a feather in his bonnet?

These were questions that would probably never have an answer, and time was awasting. He had to get back to his shelter. Spending another night out in the open was not very appealing, especially since there were Indians in the area. Where there was one, there were usually a whole passel of 'em.

He turned to leave and came face to face with a Cheyenne Indian! But it wasn't what he had expected. Here stood, not a brave, but a woman. She was quite tall and quite well shaped; from what he could tell with all the clothes she was wearing. She had a piercing gaze that seemed to look right through him, and she had a nononsense look about her. Most importantly, right now, she had an arrow knocked in her bow, and it was pointed at his heart!

Chapter Four

Dal had heard about women from some of the tribes being as fierce as any man in battle, and by the look she was giving him, he could believe it! He knew that any false move could result in his death. He didn't doubt it at all. What he did right now would determine if he lived or died. Every muscle in his body was tensed for action. Could he move quick enough to avoid the arrow? Somehow, he didn't think so. That arrow did not even waver. There wasn't even the slightest movement from her.

While Dal was thinking of his course of action, his mind was busy observing her appearance. She was slightly less than six feet tall and again he noticed how well made she was. She had clothing that had been made from the pelts of wild animals, and he noticed how well made they were also. Probably she had made them herself. Most Indians could survive on their own if they had to. Better than any white man could. He thought of his own clothes and knew they were anything but well made. She wore moccasins that had been sewn with the fur toward the foot to provide the much- needed warmth during the long winter months. The pelts used in making her overcoat and leggings had been matched before sewing and the seams were all but invisible. Only a woman would take the necessary pains to make clothes like this. He felt himself wishing he had some like those she wore!

The covering on her head was more like a hood than a hat. It fit loosely on the sides but had rawhide thongs hanging from each side and looked like they would draw the hood tight around the face when pulled on. It was totally black and contrasted with the blond hair visible around the edges. Wait a minute! BLOND HAIR! This was no Indian facing him! Her skin was a bronze color like that of an Indian, but that could happen to anyone who spent long periods of time exposed to the elements.

In spite of himself, he began to smile at her. He held his hands up, palms out, showing her he had no intentions of trying anything, and she visibly relaxed. Slowly the arrow was lowered, and Dal felt the relief of tightly strung nerves loosening all over his body. For the first time in a few minutes, he was aware of his surroundings. The sun was continuing to rise, and a jay was scolding them from a nearby tree. The little brook babbled along under the freshly fallen snow and reminded him that he was thirsty. He never took his eyes from hers, and she had blue ones, as he slowly stepped toward the stream. The arrow came back into line with his chest, and he gestured to her with his hands. Again, the bow and arrow were lowered toward the ground. Slowly he made his way to the stream and squat down. With his hand, he cupped some water to his lips and drank. He took some more and held it out to her, nodding his head at the same time.

She took two or three steps to the stream, careful to keep some distance between them. She cupped water to her mouth and drank, a smile playing on her lips. Dal was encouraged by the smile and decided to try communicating with her. He smiled back and said, "good". She nodded her head and repeated, "good".

Dal placed a hand to his chest and said, "Dal. Dal Trent." Then he held his hand out to her.

She obviously understood because she imitated him. Placing her hand on her chest, she said, "Fawn. Little Fawn."

Dal stood up and motioned for her to follow him to the campfire. He had not put the fire out, and there were still a few coals glowing. He knelt down on one knee and placed some wood on the coals. Immediately the wood caught fire and flames grew until there was a good fire going. He made a motion like he was eating, and asked, "eat?"

She smiled and nodded her head, at the same time rubbing her belly. His knapsack lay nearby, and he took out the remains of the meat, placing it on a stick and laying it over the fire. He rummaged around in the sack and found a biscuit. It was hard but chewable, and if you were hungry, which she obviously was, it would taste good. He handed it to her, and she took a bite. Her eyes lit up and she smiled the prettiest smile he had just about ever seen. Suddenly he felt awkward and uneasy. His face felt like it was burning up and he shifted his weight from one foot to another. This caused her to giggle and that only increased his uneasiness.

Abruptly she stood and walked to him, placing her hand on his arm. She looked into his eyes and said, "I'm sorry. I didn't mean to embarrass you."

The look of surprise on his face must have been obvious, for she smiled again. "You can speak English!"

"Well, I'm not an Indian if that's what you think!" she said.

"But what are you doing out here all alone in the dead of winter?" Dal asked. "And how are you staying alive?"

"I was taken from my family about five or six years ago. It's been hard to keep track of time, but I think that's about right. I was fifteen then, and we were on our way West. Pa had sold our farm back East and we were looking to make a new start wherever we could find some good soil. We were camped for the night when the war party surprised us. They killed Pa right off. He was the lucky one. Mama suffered awful when ..." Her voice trailed off as a sob escaped her lips.

"You don't have to talk about it, Little Fawn," Dal said as he placed a hand on her shoulder. "Some things are too painful to talk about. And talkin' about 'em don't change things."

"I learned to steel myself against all types of pain and humiliation I had to suffer at the hands of the Indians, but I never was able to remember what happened to my family without going to pieces. I used to get so mad with myself, because they could always get to me by bringing it up. The squaws took pleasure in seeing me cry. If it hadn't been for one brave who wanted me for his squaw, they would have probably killed me. He thought that by protecting me, I would want to be his, but that would never happen. I'd rather be dead than a squaw. Anyway, I vowed that I would someday make my escape. And here I am."

"If you made your escape, won't they be looking for you? Dal asked.

"Normally they would be, but I waited for just the right moment to make a break for it. I was allowed to go out with a hunting party, to help bring the meat back to the main camp. We were following a lone elk that had gotten separated from the herd. The trail led close to a deep ravine. When we passed it on our way in, I noticed there was a small shelf about ten feet down, that sloped

25

back under the top. It was pretty well hidden by trees and brush. The rest of the ravine dropped away for hundreds of feet. The bottom could not be seen from the trail we were on. I decided that, if at all possible, this would be my day of escape. We caught up with the elk, and the braves shot it. Soon we were loaded down with much needed meat for the village, and on our way back the way we had come, I took more than the other two squaws so it would give me an excuse to lag behind. They never seemed to question when I did this. I'm not sure why. Maybe it was because I was carrying their food. Anyway, it worked this time too. I lagged behind and when I came to the edge of the ravine, I threw the meat over the edge, and jumped down to the ledge, screaming as I went. I wasn't sure I could hold myself from going the rest of the way down, but at this point I was willing to take the chance. Death was preferable to living another day as an Indian slave. Thank God, my fall was broken by some of the branches of the pine trees, and they even pushed me in close to the rock wall, so that when I landed, I was not visible from above. I could hear their calls from above and they seemed to be more upset at losing the meat than me. I laid perfectly still for what seemed like an eternity, and they finally left. At one point though, I thought they would find me, because they were talking about sending one brave down to try and recover the meat. Thankfully, the snow proved too slippery for him to climb down. I decided I should stay put for that night because they just might have been suspicious and left someone to watch for me. I snuggled back as close as possible to the rock wall and prepared myself for a long, cold night."

"At the first hint of light, I stood up very carefully, and started to work the knots out of my muscles, knowing that one slip would mean my death."

"How in tarnation did you ever get up from there?" Dal asked in wonder. What type of woman was this in front of him anyway? Only a very special, very strong person could endure the pain of losing her family, and then having to live with the very people who had committed the atrocities. He found that as she told him of what she had been through, he was gaining more and more respect for her.

"It took me quite a while to figure it out, but as I stood there thinking all was lost, I turned toward the tree that had broken my fall, and I could see what looked like a ladder straight to the top. The limbs were spaced just right so I could climb to the top of the tree. The only thing remaining would be to jump from the tree to the ground. It was longer than any jump I had ever made before, but I knew I had to try. Up the tree I went, one branch at a time, till I was even with the ground. The tree was pretty wobbly and unsteady this far up, but I drew on all the strength I had, and on all

27

the hatred I had built up inside me against the Indians and jumped. I landed with my arms stretched out in front of me, and the edge of the ground took me right in the middle. My breath was knocked completely out of me, and I laid there hanging on for dear life. Finally, I was able to draw one leg up and get it over the top. Gradually I pulled myself up over the edge and laid there completely exhausted. It was about that time it started to snow, and I couldn't believe my good luck. They wouldn't be able to find my tracks!"

"I'm curious about one thing." Dal said." Where did you find the bow and arrows?"

"That's easy. A good Indian never goes anywhere without them. That was one of the first things they impressed on me. They were always around my neck. Most of the things I learned from them are things that will help me. I know that. It's just hard to accept anything from people who can be so cruel."

"Well, I think we should be getting back to my shelter before those Injuns stumble onto us. We've got enough trouble without that," said Dal.

"What makes you think I'm going with you?" asked Little Fawn. "I'm perfectly capable of taking care of myself."

"If you think I'm going to let you just up and leave here on your own, you're crazier than an old Loon. You'll be headin' out with me, like it or not." commanded Dal.

With flashing eyes, she turned on him, only to be met with a glare that would have withered even a seasoned mountain man. She instinctively took a step backwards, and quickly lowered her eyes. Here was a man unlike any she had ever met, and she knew it wouldn't do any good to argue with him. By the look on his face, she could see his mind was made up and there was no changing it.

"O.K., I'll go with you, but I want you to know one thing. I am not your woman or slave. And as soon as the weather permits, I'll be moving on. I don't want to be beholden to any person, man, or woman. Meanwhile, I'll do my part to help with the chores around camp. And if you're agreeable with it, I'll help run the trap line for one third the take when you sell the pelts."

"One third?! Why that's pure highway robbery!" shouted Dal. I'm the one who's risked his life to establish this trap line and you think you can just happen in here and demand a third of it?"

"Whoa, wait a minute," retorted Little Fawn. "You're the one demanding I go with you. I'm just telling you, my terms. Take em or leave em."

Had this been another man in front of him, Dal would have probably knocked his head off! As it stood, with her being a woman and all, he didn't really know what to do. This was a whole new feeling for Dal because he was usually in control of every situation.

Yet here stood a woman telling him how things were going to be!

He whirled on his heel and walked away from her. For a moment, she thought he was going to leave her here alone after all. Stopping, he stood there for a minute or two, with his back to her. Slowly he turned and faced her. Raising a hand and pointing a finger straight at her, he said, "You will do your share of the chores, and I'll decide how much you get from the sale of the pelts, after I see how much work you really do. Fair enough?"

"Fair enough," said Little Fawn.

"By the way," asked Dal." What's your real name?"

"My real name is Molly. Molly Littlefield. It was my grandmother's name on my father's side. She lived about a mile from us back home, and I used to love going to visit her. She always had fresh baked cookies or doughnuts sitting on her counter just waiting for me to sample." For a moment, a distant look came over Molly's face, but just as fast it was gone.

"Well, Molly," said Dal, pointing toward the outcropping of rock in the distance. "That is Tomahawk Ridge, and my camp is not far from there. If we get a move on, we should make it just after noon, if we don't run into any other obstacles."

"So, is that what you think I am, is an obstacle?" asked Molly with a half-smile on her face.

Dal just blushed and stooped to pick up his knap-sack and rifle. Without another word, he kicked snow over the already dying fire, and headed in the direction of Tomahawk Ridge, with Molly following close behind, taking two steps for every one of his.

Chapter Five

S everal times during the morning trek, they lost
sight of the outcropping of rock that was their
landmark, but Dal's sense of direction was flawless,
and they arrived at the base of Tomahawk Ridge shortly
before noon.

The snow had piled high during the previous storm,
and Molly's legs burned from the effort of keeping up
with the tireless pace Dal had set. She would never
have given him the pleasure of knowing that she was
having trouble, so when he asked if she wanted to take
a rest, she emphatically replied, "NO!"

"We've got about another hour before we reach
my camp," said Dal. "I want you to notice everything
around you. The rock formations, the trees, everything.
Someday you may have to get back to camp alone, and
I don't want you to have to search for it. I want you to
know where it is at all times when we are away from it.
Both our lives might well depend on how quickly you
can get back to camp. And never worry about me if we
should get separated. I can take care of myself, and if for
some reason I can't, you just worry about you. It's every

man for himself out here. And don't expect me to show you any special favors just because you're a woman."

Molly's face flamed red as she retorted, "I already told you I could take care of myself, and I don't expect any special favors. As far as worrying about you, I wouldn't even think about it!"

"Good, then follow me and pay attention," Dal shot back.

They wound their way through boulders as large as houses and twice walked on three- foot- wide ledges hundreds of feet from the valley floor. One misstep would lead to sure death on the jagged rocks below. The trail led uphill for about a mile, and then abruptly started a steep descent that ended in a valley that was surrounded by sheer rock walls on three sides. The fourth side was facing south as far as the eye could see. The beauty almost took Molly's breath away as she stood gazing out across the wide expanse of land before her.

"Pretty, huh?" asked Dal.

"That doesn't even begin to describe it," whispered Molly, as she kept her eyes riveted on the scenery before her.

"Well over here is my camp. It needs a little more work, but it's hard to tend my trap line and do work on my camp too," explained Dal.

Molly turned, half expecting to see an old half thrown together log cabin or maybe just a teepee. Her breath caught in her throat, as her eyes took in the sight before her. There was no log cabin. There was no teepee. Directly in front of her was what must have been called a castle in the days of the Crusades she had read about. The camp, as Dal had called it, was hued out of solid stone. The door was tall enough so even Dal didn't have to bend his head when he entered, and it was made of solid logs, at least eight inches thick. There was one window on each side of the door, and they each had logs covering them that could be opened up when weather permitted. Off to the right side of the camp, flowed a small stream no more than four feet from the window. Upon later inspection, Molly found as she went inside, that there was a hollowed-out log which led from the stream, through a hole in the wall of the camp, to a small rock basin that would provide fresh water at all times. On the left wall, there was a huge fireplace that would take wood four feet long. The chimney led up through a natural hole in the ceiling. Dal explained to Molly later that the smoke was dissipated through a series of smaller holes that eventually led to the top of the rock formation. This, he explained must have been done by water from the stream that now ran beside the camp. Because of this, the smoke was not noticeable from anywhere on the top.

As Molly let her eyes roam around the room, she was impressed with the furniture that was in the room. There was a table and four chairs in the middle of the room, a bench that sat against the wall by the door, and a large bed in the corner near the fireplace.

Dal broke the silence and told Molly to get her things inside while he went to fetch some meat for their evening meal. "I've got a stash of meat not far from here. If you want to start a fire, I'll get the meat and we'll eat as soon as it's ready."

Molly had a roaring fire going when Dal got back, and it was already warm enough on the inside so they didn't have to wear their coats.

Dal plopped the hind quarter of venison down and proceeded to carve a generous portion and place it on the spit to roast. Molly had already placed some water in the iron kettle over the fire and Dal got out some coffee. As he put some water in the coffee pot and added the coffee, Molly asked him about how he had come to have such a wonderful place.

"Well, I wish I could take all the credit for it, but I can't. I stumbled on to it one day when I was scoutin' out the area. It was just pure chance that I found it at all. I was trackin' a deer, and he led me down the very path we just came down. When I saw all this, I could hardly believe my eyes! A luckier man has never lived! I knew right then and there that this was my new home. I started makin' furniture, right off. There had to be new logs for the doors and winders, cause the others were rotted and gone. I knew by the look of the place, there hadn't been anybody here for a long spell. I've still got some more things to do to make it more comfortable, 'especially now that you're here."

"Don t think you have to show any special courtesies to me," said Molly, her eyes flashing.

"Don t think I am," Dal shot back. "I'm only thinkin' of me. If you think I'll be sleepin' on the floor the rest of the winter, you are about as loony as one of them ole Injun squaws you been livin' with! Tomorrow mornin', I'll be makin' me a new bed, so's you can sleep on that one yonder. So, don' t think I'm doin' you no favors!"

Molly had to stifle a smile, because even though Dal said he wasn't thinking of her, she could see that in truth, he really was. He was prepared to sleep on the floor until a new bed could be made. Deep down, she really appreciated all that he was sacrificing just to help her. She knew that a man of his caliber had rather be left alone out here in the wilderness. She was sorry that she had intruded on him like this. She would not be a burden to him, and as soon as she was able, she would move on. Where, she had no idea. She supposed she could always go back to her grandmother, but she really liked this country out here. Why did she have to be a woman anyway?

Dal's thoughts at this moment were somewhere, but he didn't rightly know where. He tried to busy himself with tending to the meat and putting away his supplies from his pack. He didn't know what the matter was with him, getting all flustered over nothing. He was always taught to respect a woman, and to be a gentleman around them. He didn't know why she was getting all worked up! And was that a trace of a smile on her face? Why in tarnation was she laughing at him? Women!!

The meat was done cooking and so they each sat down at the table to eat. It was a surprise to both of them to see the other bow their head for grace. Nothing however was said, and the meal was eaten in silence. The coffee was ready, and Molly poured each of them a cupful. Dal muttered his thanks and retreated to one corner of the room to sit in silence, while Molly took water from the pot in the fireplace and washed the dishes.

Darkness was fast approaching, and Dal lit the kerosene lamp. A warm light emanated from the fireplace and the lamp and bathed the whole place in a homey atmosphere. They both began to feel the effects of their long trek in the deep snow and the warmth of the fire. Their eyelids began to droop, and their heads began to nod.

"You take the bed and I'll sleep here on the floor." Dal said as he threw a few furs in the corner near the fireplace. Molly didn't argue, as she stood, stretched, and walked to the bed. She climbed under the furs that had been sewn together for blankets and within minutes Dal could tell she was asleep by her slow and steady breathing. He was thinking of all the day had brought his way when he too fell into a deep restful sleep.

The sun had just begun its journey, with a few rays poking their way over the park in front of the cold rock walls of the place that Dal Trent, and now Molly Littlefield, called home. The freshly fallen snow glittered with a million diamonds as the sun slowly spread its light over the earth. The wind was silent, and the air crisp. It was one of those mornings that made you glad to be alive.

Dal was already more than two miles from home, checking his trapline. He already knew there would not be much, if anything, in the traps today. The animals seemed to know when a storm would hit, and they tended to lay low. And with about two feet of new snow on top of his traps, even if an animal stepped on one, it wouldn't trigger it. The only hopes he had of catching anything today would be in the beaver traps that were set under the water. All in all, he had about seven or eight miles of trapline to check each day. Many trappers didn't check their lines every day and some only checked them once a week. Dal had seen some animals caught by the leg for days on end. Some even chewed their own leg off to get free. He had vowed never to let any animals caught by him go through any unnecessary suffering. He also never trapped more than one season in one area. He always allowed time for the animals to replenish their numbers before trapping there again. This way he was always assured of a good season, and he hadn't been disappointed yet. Sometimes it meant a longer walk, but he knew it was worth it.

As he busied himself with the task at hand, of resetting the traps on top of the snow, his thoughts went back to the woman that now occupied his home with him. She was certainly about the biggest surprise he had ever gotten in his whole entire life! He didn't quite know how to take her. She was unlike any other female he had ever encountered. He was impressed to say the least. She was not whiney like some of the girls back home had been. Whenever something had gone wrong, they were always crabbing and, well, acting like girls! This girl didn't act like a girl. She acted more like him. She could take care of herself. She sure could be exasperating though! And for no apparent reason. He guessed he was glad she would only be staying 'til Spring.

Molly slowly became aware of her surroundings as she opened her eyes and looked around. The fire was still going, and she thought that was odd. Could it have gone all night? The smell of coffee was strong and for a moment, she thought maybe she had only been asleep for a little while. But the lamp was not lit, and daylight was evident through the cracks between the logs in the door. She slowly turned over and glanced over to the corner where Dal had made his bed last night, only to find it empty. He was gone and so were the furs. She bounded out of bed and opened the door to a gorgeous morning. The sun hit her full in the face and for a moment blinded her. She shaded her eyes and looked around for signs of Dal, all the while listening for sounds that might reveal to her his whereabouts. After a moment, she noticed fresh tracks heading down through the park and realized that Dal had gotten an early start. She was surprised and impressed that he had managed to build up the fire, make coffee, and leave without her even hearing the slightest rustle. She decided she would have to be more alert from now on.

Going back inside, she shut the door to keep the cold out, and poured herself a cup of hot coffee. It was strong tasting but warmed her from the inside out. She decided this place needed a woman's touch and began thinking of ways she could improve on an already comfortable quarters. As she began to straighten up the bed covers where she had slept, she noticed how poorly sewn together the furs were. It had obviously been done by a man! That would be a good place to start. First, she had to locate the materials she needed. Slowly she looked round the room and eventually her eyes came to rest on a small box that was half hidden under some small pieces of tanned leather in a far corner of the room. She walked to the corner, and after moving the pieces of leather, she picked the box up and opened the cover. Inside was a needle made of bone and some sinew that was used in the place of thread. She was very familiar with the use of these objects because this had been one of her many tasks she had had to perform while living in the Indian village. She had actually gotten quite good at it even if she did say so herself. She had even gotten so she could match skins together, so the seam was barely noticeable. Because of this, she had been forced to do much of the sewing in the village, but she had come to realize there were many jobs that were far worse than this. And so, she had welcomed the work.

Molly set about taking the furs apart that had been so haphazardly sewn together and smiled to herself as she pictured Dal struggling through this type of work. He would probably despise doing it, and that would explain why it was not done very well. She would have a surprise for him when he got home tonight.

Chapter Six

Dal Trent was indeed an extraordinary man. His upbringing had been by people who were good moral people. He had been taught the difference between right and wrong. He respected other peoples' rights, and he would never knowingly do anything that would hurt someone else, unless that person was trying to hurt him or someone he cared about. All mountain men were not cut from the same material. Though most lived by an unspoken creed, there were some who lived by their own rules. Some who didn't care who or what they hurt as long as they got what they wanted.

About twenty miles Northwest of Dal's camp, there was just such a group of scoundrels. Five in number, they had made their way South over the last few days. They had joined company at the start of winter and had failed to lay in stores enough to last all season. So now they were without supplies, and they were looking for anything they could lay their hands on. The storms had made it hard to locate any game, and they were hungry, cold, and about in as good a mood as an old sow grizzly separated from her cub. They rode along in silence, except for the occasional curse or belittlement thrown out at the one in front to get a move on.

How they had come to be together, was really quite an accident. Two of them, Frank Williams, and Jake Miller, the most experienced in the bunch, had ridden together for six or eight years. They had spent most of their time in the mountains, but most of the furs they collected every year were stolen from some other trapper s line. They would find where a trapper was working, and then they would work on the far end of the trapper s circle, so they had less chance of being caught. So far, it had worked quite well. They had only had to kill two trappers. The way they figured it was if the trappers had left them alone, everything would have been all right. There was no remorse for any of their actions. In their minds, they had done nothing wrong. Those unlucky enough to suffer their wrath would not be missed anyhow. Most trappers were loners, without much, if any, family back home. And even if they did have family, they almost never contacted them. When they left home, they were usually gone for good. No one would miss them.

The other three were all younger men who had come to the mountains to try and make a name for themselves. They had all three grown up in the same locale. They had all three been illtempered young men who had gotten into trouble with the law, and they thought going to the mountains would make people respect them. In reality, the people who knew them were more than happy to see them leave. They hoped they would never have to put up with them again.

Wayne and John Evans were brothers, and Bill Marsh had been close to them during the time they had grown up. In fact, they had lived just one town over from where Dal Trent had lived. It was the talk they heard about how brave Dal had been to leave home and head for the great unknown, that had prompted them to set out for the Rockies. They remembered well the unsettled business they had with Mr. Dal Trent. Maybe if they were lucky, they'd meet up with him out here where they didn't have to worry about the law!

It had certainly been by chance that these five had met. If any of them had met up with anyone else, they would certainly not have formed a partnership with them. Wayne, John, and Bill saw in Frank and Jake, a chance to team up with someone who had already gained experience in mountain living. Frank and Jake saw in the other three, a chance to maybe order them to do their dirty work for them.

It had not gone well for them since they had banded together. Every one of them wanted to be the chief of this tribe. Every one of them was forever telling the rest what to do. It was because of this, that their winter supplies were lacking. Not one of them would do the work it required to lay in the winter stores of wood and food. Now they were paying for it, and of course it was everyone else's fault.

They continued to drift South hoping to run into some unsuspecting trapper who maybe had done a better job laying in on supplies. The horses they were riding, although they were fine looking animals in the fall, while they were able to graze on the lush grass in the mountain meadows, were now gaunt and weak. Still the men continued to push them relentlessly. They wouldn't think of walking as long as there was a horse standing.

"Cain't you varmints move any fester?" Jake called from the rear.

"Maybe you just ought'n to come up yar and show us'n how it's done, you big mountain man!" Bill shot back.

"If'n y'all had done what I told yer to, we wouldn't be in this here predicament," shouted Frank. "We might jest hafta shoot one of you boys fer food fer too long!"

This prompted looks to be exchanged between the three and brought cackles from the other two. The boys didn't know if they meant it or not, but they didn't trust them with a dog's dinner.

They made about five miles before the horses were not able to go any farther. They decided to dismount and lead their mounts for the rest of the day, which was fast fading into twilight. It looked like another bonechilling

45

night was ahead of them, and they knew if shelter was not found, it could be dangerous. Especially since they hadn't eaten much for the past few days.

The men plodded along through the snow, that was kneehigh, and the horses reluctantly followed. Given a choice, the horses would have stopped right then and there. They were always able to dig through the snow and find at least some sustenance, which gave them an advantage over the men. Though it in no way would allow them to gain, they could at least crop enough grass to maintain their daily requirement. The men were in an entirely different situation. If they didn't find food, and find it fast, they would begin to lose strength rapidly. Their eyes were constantly moving, taking in even the smallest details of their surroundings.

The land sloped up sharply from where they had just come and was now beginning to level off. Trees were becoming thicker here, and their senses were on full alert. There should be some kind of game here. They could almost taste a nice, thick, juicy, deer or elk steak. Just before they entered the thickest of the trees, Frank spoke to the others in a hushed whisper.

"You boys want I should sneak in there ahead, and see if I can rustle up some varmint for our supper?"

There was a moment of exchanged glances, then a unanimous nod of approval.

46

"I want yous to keep these here horses quiet, Bill. And I want the rest of you to spread out and keep them eyeballs peeled. You never know what might be in this here thicket. Give me a minute or two to go in, and then you boys come in too, only don t shoot me!" whispered Frank. "The wind is about right, and I'm a thinkin' there must be sumpin in thar."

Slowly, Frank turned and stalked his way into the thickest of the spruce trees. The foliage seemed to swallow him up. One second, he was there, and the next he had vanished. Glances were exchanged again, among the four remaining. Bill took the reins from the other men and was secretly glad he didn't have to participate in this little hunt.

John, Jake, and Wayne spread out into a line, and Jake gave the signal to advance. As one, they started into the tangle of brush and trees, and as one they all vanished, just as Frank had done. Bill's mind began to work as soon as he lost sight of his comrades, and he then wished he wasn't left here all alone to watch the horses. He'd heard tales told where men had just up and disappeared into thin air. What would he do out here all alone in this vast expanse of God forsaken wilderness? How would he ever find food all by himself? What would he do if he encountered Indians? He could never defend himself against more than four or five of those savages. And he certainly didn't relish the thought of being caught and tortured by those heathens. He'd heard plenty of stories about that too. Too many in fact. Oh, if he could just be in there with the rest of them, he would feel so much better. He began to look around like he expected to see an Indian behind every tree. The light was slowly fading, and shadows were playing tricks with his eyes. There was movement everywhere.

This, however, was entirely in his mind. The horses, who could always be counted upon to let you know if anyone or anything was around, were quietly standing with their heads hanging low, indeed almost asleep.

Frank made his way through the tangle as quietly as he could, eyes constantly searching. He had almost made it to the center of the thicket, when he caught a glimpse of something that made him stop. Off to the right, and about thirty yards away, he could just make out what looked to be like the hind quarter of a deer. It was getting quite dark in here, and it was hard to be one hundred per cent sure. He would have to stand still and see if he could detect any movement. He could vaguely begin to hear the other men advancing through the brush, and he hoped they wouldn't spook the deer, if indeed that was what it was.

Sure enough! He saw the deer's tail flick. The rifle slowly came to his shoulder, and he sighted down the length of the barrel. Slowly his finger tightened on the trigger. The stillness of the evening air was interrupted by the roar of the musket, and through the smoke he could see a lot of movement now. He would wait a few minutes and see if his shot proved true. He hoped the others would not come running up to see what he had shot at. They had hunted together enough so they should know what to do.

He still saw some movement, so he knew his shot had been accurate, at least enough so to render the deer helpless. Now he could finish it off and they would dine like royalty tonight.

Almost automatically, he had reloaded his rifle after his shot. You don't live long out here if you forget to load as soon as possible. He made his way to where the deer had been thrashing around. It was all but still now, so he decided to not waste any more powder. Once again, he could hear his partners coming up behind him, and he made a sound like an owl. Immediately this call was answered in the exact way, and in less than two shakes of a deer s tail, they were standing around admiring the kill, their mouths fairly watering in anticipation of the meal to come.

Back behind them, they could hear Bill calling to them, and he sounded frantic. They decided they had better get out there and see what was wrong, so Frank told the others to go check on him.

"I'll stay here and start making camp, whilst you boys go rescue ol' Bill. Sounds like he's had too long a time to think agin. I swear that ol coon sounds like he's done gone off his rocker! Hehehe."

By the time they had gotten Bill calmed down and explained to him that Frank had shot a nice, fat, deer, and had found a path clear enough to get the horses through, Frank had some firewood stacked. He then set about cutting off some choice pieces of venison and spitting them on sticks to roast over the fire.

It didn't take any time at all before the coals were ready for cooking, seeing as how there was plenty of dry wood at hand, and before long they were settled down filling their hungry faces with juicy deer meat. Talk was at a bare minimum, and it wasn't until after they had eaten their fill, did they get around to asking Bill what had set him off so. Jake was the first to bring it up. Bill had silently been hoping it had been forgotten, but knew it was too much to hope for.

"What in tarnation was you squealing like a stuck pig fer back thar?" Jake wanted to know. "Sounded like the whole Blackfeet nation was after ya," he teased.

"You just keep yer mouth shet about me. Besides there ain't no Blackfeet around these parts. How was I to know what was ahappnin in here, I couldn't even see ya after ya' d gone ten steps. Even the hosses was a acting skittish, like there was somthin' around," Bill fired back.

Frank had about had his fill of the way Bill reacted to being alone, and he said," I don't want to hear one more word from any of ya. Bill, if you ever act that way agin when I'm huntin , I'll shoot you fust. I swear it on my dead pappy's grave. Now let's get some shuteye. I want us to be out of here by sunup".

With that, they kicked back on their bedrolls and dozed off.

Chapter Seven

Morning dawned bright and sunny, and they breakfasted on more deer meat. There would be a small portion left from the kill and they could pack that in their saddlebags with no problem.

John was the first one to speak." Where 'bouts we headin' today, Frank?"

Frank eyed him and was in no hurry to answer. Silence lasted for about five minutes, and John was about to ask again when Frank spoke. "I reckon we'll just keep on headin' South till we run on ta somthin'. Thar s got to be some fool trapper down this way somewheres. We'll jest relieve him of some of his furs till he cetches on, and then we'll relieve him of his scalp. We'll let him do the work for as long as we can. Jest keep an eye on him, so we know when he s gittin spicious, then." With this he drew his thumb across his throat so there was no doubt what his intentions were. Malicious grins were spread around, and nothing more was said until the meal was done. Each was lost in his own thoughts of what they might find in the camp of their next victim. They might even find gold. Some old trappers found gold in the streams they trapped in and just hoarded it away. And maybe, just maybe, they would be lucky enough to find a squaw in that camp! It had been a long time since they had even seen a woman, let alone touched one.

Jake broke the dream by saying, "We best be hittin' the trail, if' n we're a goin' ta be findin' this here trapper."

They all readily agreed, and set about rolling up their blankets, tying them to their saddles, and then throwing the saddles on their horses. The horses, being rested now, were eager to be going. They could almost sense they were heading in a direction where they could more easily find grass without having to dig through as much snow. And so once again, the small company of roughnecks headed in a Southerly direction in their quest for easy money.

They had ridden for the better part of the day, not even stopping for lunch, when Frank, who was in the lead, held up his hand for them to halt. In the snow ahead of them was a small stand of spruce trees, and a trail of some sort leading into them. Frank put his finger to his mouth, in a sign for silence, and he quietly slipped off his mount. He checked the load in his musket and pistol, and then slowly made his way toward the trees. As his path crossed the one that he had seen, he could make out that there were two sets of tracks. One was extremely large, and the other was quite small.

53

He went to a crouching position, and resumed his stalk of the thicket. He wasn't sure if they were still in there, but he wasn't taking any chances either. He might be in the sights of a rifle right now!

The other four sat their horses but readied their rifles in case the need arose to use them. They hardly blinked as they watched their leader making his way ever so slowly along the snowy path.

When Frank reached the edge of the thicket, he could almost see right through to the other side, it was that small. He let his eyes drift from one end to the other, and, satisfied there was no one still here, he motioned for the others to ride up. He stepped into the trees and found a hole in the snow where a campfire had burned, and where some giant of a man had evidently spent the night. From there, he looked to his right, and saw the frozen, skinned, carcass of a wolf. Upon closer inspection, he found where an arrow had penetrated the heart. The arrow was no longer there, but nevertheless it was an arrow hole, and arrows mean Indians. His eyes narrowed to slits as he tried to read the sign as it lay before him. What had gone on here?

His eyes picked up another set of tracks, the smaller ones he had found outside the thicket, right next to the larger ones, but no evidence showed that whoever had made those tracks, had spent the night in this camp. They came in to the camp from a different angle, and as he followed them, he soon found where the snow was packed down behind an old uprooted tree. It appeared this person, man or woman, had spent the night here in hiding, but why? Was the giant being hunted? And what about the dead wolf with the arrow hole? These questions and more flashed through his mind as he waited for the others to make their way to him. They didn't seem too eager to advance, not knowing what to expect, so Frank gave the usual owl call to let them know that all was well. It was answered immediately, and soon they were standing beside Frank.

"I don't know what in tarnation went on here, but It sure looks powerful strange," Frank stated quietly, almost in a whisper.

"Why for you be whisperin Frank?" asked Wayne. "You spect somebody's still in earshot?"

"Naw, tain't likely," said Frank, still whispering. "But somethins sure strange here. I cain't figgir it out. Thars an arrow hole in thet thar wolf, but thar don't pear to be no sign of a tussle, or anythin'." And the tracks lead off South with the littler ones in the bigger ones. Did you ever see any bigger tracks than these boys? I thought I had big feet, but they ain't nowhere near the size of these. With this, Frank stepped his foot alongside the track in the snow for comparison. The others crowded around to see and couldn't believe their eyes. This track dwarfed the size of Frank's foot, and Frank wasn't a small man!

"What you make of all this, Frank? queried Bill. "Are we a goin ta follar um? Looks like that little track might've been made by a woman. You reckon that biggun is a Injun?"

"I say that track is too big fer it to be a Injun," Jake injected. "I think that small one must be the Injun. Maybe his squaw."

"O.K. smarty pants, then why did she spend the night over behind that blowdown?" asked John. Why didn't she warm his robes for him there by the fire? No selfrespectin' redblooded trapper goin' ta be leavin' her out thar in the cold."

Jake turned to Frank. "We goin ta follar em? It appears thar headin' in the same direction as we is."

Frank took his time and inspected the area once more. He slowly turned to the rest of them and said, "I reckon we'll spend the night right here. In the mornin', we'll find out what this here coon is up to."

Morning was about as cold as these boys had seen in their time in the mountains. The temperature was hovering at about minus thirty, and the wind was blowing hard enough to set the snow to drifting. Traveling was difficult even in normal circumstances, with snow about three feet deep. Now the drifts were nearing six feet in places. Deep enough so that a horse could get bogged down and require someone to dig him out. The trail they had thought would be so easy to follow, was now nigh to impossible to keep in sight. Tempers were flaring and each blamed the other for their circumstances, though they never came right out and said it.

They continued to plod along in the general direction the tracks had pointed but were unsure if they were still on the trail. Bill was the first to speak in hours. "Frank, how long we goin ta keep on in this here blizzard? My horse is 'bout wore out, and I'm gittin' a powerful hunger on."

"We'll stop when I says we stop. We only got bout one more hour fore sundown. We'll build camp whar ever thar's shelter from this here wind," shouted Frank over the moan of the wind. He had noticed the horses were pretty near winded and he was getting pretty hungry himself, but now that one of the others had mentioned stopping to him, he'd be durned if he would stop now. They would stop when he said they would stop!

The other men kept their silence but exchanged glances among themselves. Frank was getting way too big for his own britches. If he thought he could just tell them what to do all the time, well, that was going to change.

About another half mile, they came upon a small clump of trees that offered a meager shelter from the wind. Since there didn't seem to be anything else around that was any better, they made camp here. Darkness was falling fast, as they lit a small fire, gradually adding wood to make a roaring fire that would warm their chilled bodies and roast their supper of deer meat. As soon as they had taken care of their horses, they all sat around the fire in silence and ate. Then one by one, they rolled in their blankets and robes and were soon snoring, oblivious to the howling wind and blowing snow.

Chapter Eight

About five miles away, in the shelter of the canyon, the wind was barely noticeable. Molly had expected Dal to come back that evening, but he hadn't showed up. She had sat up waiting for him for a while, then decided it was a waste of her time to worry about a man she had just met and didn't have any interest in whatsoever. She crawled under the new robes she had finished sewing and repairing and settled in for a nice sleep. As she began to drift off to sleep, her thoughts involuntarily turned to the man who seemed larger than life, and a smile crossed her face. She had never met anyone like him, and yet there was something familiar about him. She was sure she had never seen him before, but he certainly looked familiar. She told herself she was being silly, and with that, she drifted off to sleep.

Three miles down the park, from the shelter, Dal huddled near a blazing fire, wrapped in a buffalo robe. His eyes were heavy from the hard day's work of tramping through the snow checking the trap line. All in all, it had been a good days catch. He had found two silver foxes, three bobcats, and one wolf. The furs were prime and would bring a good price at the trading post next spring. If all went well, he would have enough money to lay in next year's supplies with a little to spare.

His eyes slowly closed, and his thoughts went back up the valley to the shelter, where the most beautiful woman he had ever seen slept right now. A slow smile crept over his face, and he drifted off to sleep.

Next morning, the wind had died down and the sun made its way over the distant ridges with a brightness that seemed to explode. Dal had never ceased to be amazed at how one moment there was only gray, and the next moment the light was so bright it almost blinded you.

With good luck today, he would be back to the shelter by nighttime. He could have made it back last night, but he had dawdled here and there, telling himself he had to do this, and he had to do that. In reality, he was a little shy around Molly. He had never been really comfortable around girls when he was growing up, and It seemed it was even worse now. Especially around Molly. Well, he guessed he'd just have to get over it, 'cause it looked like she was going to be around at least for the rest of the winter. He certainly wasn't going to spend the rest of the winter half freezing to death around an open fire! With thoughts of that kind, he headed in the direction of the shelter.

All went smoothly on his way back up the valley, and the trap line was paying off handsomely. As he came in view of his home, he could see the all familiar surroundings he had gotten so used to seeing on his return from the many trips he made checking the trap line. This time, however, he noticed something different. As he got closer, he could make out a lone figure in front of the shelter busy with something. He recognized her, and immediately felt a little warmer inside. His pace quickened, and in no time at all, he was standing in front of her with his pack of furs.

Molly had seen him coming up the valley, and even though she would not have admitted it, she was glad to see him. She had been a little worried last night when he hadn't come home, being as cold as it was. She knew if he had fallen and broken a leg or something, he might freeze in a matter of hours.

Now he was home, and everything seemed to be as It should be. She was conscious of a jay calling nearby, and the sunlight filtering down through the trees. As he drew nearer, she pretended not to see him, and continued to spread the furs on the ground to air out.

Dal stopped about fifteen feet away from her. "Mornin' Molly," he said.

Molly's head came up, and a slow smile spread across her face. "Mornin', Dal. You're a little late coming back. Any trouble?"

Dal continued to stare at her, and he saw a redness begin low on her neck and travel slowly up her face into her hairline. He also was aware that his face seemed a little warmer than usual. "No, I just was busy with the trap line and kind of lost track of time 'til it was too dark to make it back. I did real good though. The traps gave us some real nice furs".

The fact that he had used the word us was not lost on her, and secretly she was pleased that he would accept her as a partner as easily as he had.

"Were ya worried about me?" Dal asked, with a smile playing on his lips.

"Not one bit, Molly shot back, I just didn't want to have to dig a hole fer your old carcass, what with this frozen ground and all. And I sure wouldn't want to have to store ya till Spring!"

Dal took the pelts over to the bench he had built and tossed them in the corner next to the rock wall of the cliff that towered at least fifty feet over their heads. He had made the bench especially for the purpose of fleshing and stretching the pelts, and all the tools he needed were within arm's reach. After they were stretched, he would hang them up to dry. He was well practiced, and the whole process didn't take very long at all. He was very careful during the skinning process, and so he had very little meat to remove when he got back to camp. He had learned over the years, many little steps that saved him lots of time. He used these steps without even thinking about them anymore. Out here, a man either learned or he died. It was that simple. Dal had been one to learn quickly, and he loved this life. He loved everything about his life and would not give it up for anything.

He grinned at the remark Molly had made as he set about his work and thought about how good It seemed to have someone around to talk to. He hadn't really thought he would ever want anyone here with him, but now it seemed sort of natural like. Molly continued busying herself with chores around the camp, and the hours passed swiftly. The sun was beginning to sag in the West when they both neared completion of the work they were doing.

Dal took an armful of wood and dumped it inside near the fire. He added a couple of pieces to the dying embers and the flames began to grow again. It was still warm inside and as the heat began to seep in, Dal began to feel how tired he really was. Molly came inside and threw the furs that she had aired out, back on top of the bed.

"I just realized that I'm so hungry I could eat a full growed grizzly bar," Dal said as he looked over at Molly.

"You git me some meat, and I'll cook us up some supper," Molly chuckled.

Dal threw on his coat. "I'll be back shortly," he tossed over his shoulder as he went out the door. In just about five minutes he was back with a piece of meat that looked like maybe it was a small grizzly! He took the spit he had made for just such occasions and pushed it through the meat. Then he sat it over the fire where it began to sizzle and pop, as the juice dripped into the coals. Molly turned the spit, so it got evenly cooked, and in no time at all, they were cutting off thick juicy slices of Elk meat.

Molly ate more than she ever recalled eating before, and Dal ate more than she thought possible for one man to eat! There was nothing left of the roast when he was done.

With the combination of having their bellies full, and the warmth of the fire, they were ready to call it a day. Dal stood up and said to Molly, "you get ready for bed. I'll go outside while you get undressed."

"O. K.," Molly answered. "It will only take me a minute."

Dal went outside and closed the door, while Molly got undressed and put on her soft doeskin robe, she had made while living with the Indians. She had always liked the softness of it next to her skin and had taken to wearing it as a nightdress. She next combed out her hair and let it fall over her shoulders.

Outside, Dal was listening to the night sounds. An owl hooted in the distance. A wolf howled from off down the valley, and the sound echoed up over the rock walls, sending a shiver up Dal s back. From within Molly called for him to come back inside. The wind was stirring from North to South tonight, and as he turned to go, the smell of smoke caught his attention immediately. He stopped dead and sniffed the air. For anyone to have seen him, it would have reminded them of a dog trying to get the scent of something. Small intakes of breath through the nostrils. The smell was gone, but he was certain it had been there. He opened the door and stepped inside with a look of concern on his face. Molly immediately knew that something was bothering him. That look was unmistakable.

"What's wrong Dal?" She asked, concern showing in her face and in her voice.

"I smelled smoke outside just now. It was there for just a moment and then it was gone," Dal answered. It was easy to see he was more than just a little concerned.

"It was probably just from our own fire," reasoned Molly.

"Molly, I've lived here long enough to know when I can smell smoke from this fire and when I can't. This is one of those times when I can't. The wind is coming from the wrong direction for that to be the case. It has something to do with the rock formation. When the wind comes from the North like it is tonight, it's impossible to smell smoke from this fire."

"You said yourself that this place is almost impossible to get to if you don t know the trail in. Nobody will bother us in here, Dal." Molly tried her best to sound confident. She wanted to believe in the worst way that she had nothing to fear from the Indians she had been forced to live with. But try as she might, her voice still held a slight tremor as she spoke.

"We're at least safe for the night. No man in his right mind would try to negotiate that trail in the pitch dark," Dal offered. "We can get a good night s sleep and see what the morning brings."

With that, he blew out the lantern and settled in the corner on a pile of skins with a sigh. Molly climbed into bed under the pile of furs, feeling guilty for taking his bed and making him sleep on the floor.

Soon, the room that was hewn out of stone, was filled with the sounds of snores from the pile of skins in the corner.

Chapter Nine

Morning broke cold and clear, except for a few wispy clouds in the East. Dal was up; had been before the sun and was ready to start his long trek along the trap line once more. He was restless and did not want to leave Molly here by herself after last night. Something nagged at him, but he wasn't sure what. He was never one to borrow trouble, and he knew that under most circumstances, Molly could take care of herself. She had been through a lot, and he knew she was a very capable woman. Throwing his pack on his back, he turned from looking down the valley, and went through the door to the warmth within. Molly was up and was busying herself with things that only a woman could see needed doing. She looked up as he entered and smiled. She could still see the worry on his face.

"Dal are you still thinking about that smoke last night? I don't think we have anything to worry about. Whoever it was, they were probably only passing through and are long gone by now."

"Nobody just passes through this time of year, Molly. You should know that. Anyone out in the open up here, is there for a reason. With this amount of snow and with all this cold weather, most people would be holed up for the winter. Either they didn't plan very well, and didn't have enough supplies, or they are out seeing what they can plunder from others. Either way, it stacks up as trouble. I'm not sure I want to leave you here alone. Why don t you come with me today? That way I can keep an eye on you and show you how to tend the traps just in case you have to some time. Sort of killing two birds with one stone. What do you say?"

"Well, I'm not sure," Molly answered uncertainly. She turned her back and thought for a moment. Turning to face him, she said with an edge in her voice, "I'm not afraid to stay here, and don t you think that for one second! I've handled Injuns before, and I think I could handle most anything that could come my way. So don't you go offering to take me with you just cause you think I'm scared!"

"Molly, I know you can handle more than most women. Fact is, I think you can handle more than most men, but I'm not sure who might be out there. How many there are or what type of men, God only knows. I've known some pretty rough characters from these parts. Most are trustworthy, but then you can always find some who aren't. If these are some of those who aren't, you wouldn't be safe for one minute with them. Most haven t seen a woman for a long time, and they tend to forget there are two types of women, those who will and those who won't. They classify all women as those who will. You wouldn't stand a chance with them. I think it would be good if you came with me. I'd like to show you what's down the valley."

She looked straight into his eyes as if searching for any sign of falsehood. Their eyes locked and held for a long moment. He was glad he had been truthful with her, for he could sense that she would not budge if she thought he had been lying to her.

In reality, he was concerned for her safety and felt he needed to protect her. He also knew the trap line had to be checked on a regular basis, and so this would make it possible for him to do both at the same time. Overall, a good arrangement, he thought.

She was the first to look away, and she went straight for her pack in the corner. She took it, along with her bow and quiver full of arrows and laid them on the bed. Then she dressed herself for the harsh weather they might encounter. Elk skin moccasins with the fur turned in for warmth, leggings of the same, and coat made from the hide of a great bear that had been given to her by one of the young bucks who fancied her for himself. She slung the pack on her back, which contained things she might need in emergencies, such as jerked meat, pemmican, (a mixture of dried meat that was pounded into a paste and mixed with fat and berries for flavor and made into small cakes,) and dried moss and shavings to aid in the starting of fires.

Picking up her bow and arrows she turned toward the door, and as she walked out, she said over her shoulder, "What are you waiting for white man? Let's go!"

Dal couldn't help but chuckle as he followed her through the door, closing it behind him, but only after taking one last look around to make sure how things were left. Dal retrieved his rifle and supplies, along with a pair of snowshoes for each of them should they get caught in the deep show. Being prepared for what might happen, made it possible for you to see tomorrow's sunrise.

The sun was just peeking over the horizon to the East as they began their day long journey down the valley. The snow sparkled with a million diamonds and the air was clean and fresh. The wind was still, and the snow crunched under their feet. Off in the distance a jay began to squawk and complain as they invaded his territory. They would walk in silence, for both pairs of ears were listening for any sound that was out of place; both pair of eyes were searching for movement that was foreign to their wilderness surroundings.

Both Dal and Molly felt good to be out doing what they each had come to love doing most. They loved being a part of this huge, wild, country. Both knew deep down, if given the choice of dying here or going back to civilization, they would choose death without hesitation.

Chapter Ten

Northwest of this valley by about five miles, in a small grove of softwoods, five men huddled in their blankets against the cold. The fire was all but out, and no one had bothered to gather any extra wood before retiring for the night. The horses were standing off to one side, their heads drooped low, ribs showing for lack of sufficient food.

One by one the men came awake, as the sun began its slow crawl up the rocky landscape. One by one they rolled out of their blankets and waited for someone else to build up the fire.

"Bill, you go fetch some wood fer this here fire," Frank growled. "Wayne, you git the rest of that meat outn them thar saddlebags. We got to have breakfast and git back on the trail of this here giant."

Bill shot a look at Frank that was laced with pure hatred. He hated to be ordered around like some slave. If he only could make it to Springtime, he'd be long gone from these parts. Grumbling to himself, he got to his feet and went in search of some wood dry enough to burn. Wayne took his time getting up, and then stood painstakingly folding his blanket, looking off over the landscape. He, having finished folding the blanket, then sauntered over to where the saddles were thrown in a heap and took the meat out of one of the saddlebags.

"Next time you want something," growled Wayne, "you better be sure you want it bad enough to get it yourself!"

At about the same time, Bill came back carrying an armload of wood, which he threw on the ground at Frank's feet. "I figure thet about does it fer me. I ain't nobodies' slave, and I don't take orders from no half froze coon who's too lazy to do fer his self! Next time you want wood, you jest feel free to go git it!" He spat a long brown stream of tobacco juice onto the toe of Frank's boot.

"Why you two lazy, good fer nuthins, I ought to blow a hole in the both of ya. If'n twern't fer ol John and me, you other three would be long dead by now. Why don t you jest go yer own way, and Jake and me'll git along jest fine. I got a feelin the Injuns are wishin they had some sport right about now. Mebbe you three could provide that for em." With that Frank leveled his pistol at Bill and double cocked it. Bill's eyes doubled in size and an instant sweat broke out on his face. To be staring down the business end of that old flintlock at such close range, was not his idea of fun and games.

Jake had ridden long enough with Frank to know when he meant business and when he was bluffing. Right now, he knew that he was all business. He also knew that if he killed Bill, that would leave them with one less gun should they run up against something unexpected. Frank always tended to shoot first and think later. Jake always had to do the thinking for them whenever Frank got this way, and right now he was thinking this wasn't a good idea. He was sitting about two feet away from where Frank now stood, but he knew that he could never reach that gun before it went off. It had a hair trigger and just the slightest jar would set it off.

"Frank are you sure you want to do this right now?" asked Jake. "You could at least wait 'til after we find this here giant we're trailin'. After that you can do whatever, you see fit to do."

"I ain't waitin' fer nothin'. It's time we was rid of this scum." He extended his arm closer to Bill, and Jake knew this was it. Jake rolled into Frank's legs, knocking him off balance. The gun roared, and Bill fell to the ground clutching his left arm.

"What in tarnation did ya do that fer? bellowed Frank. Now he's not only lazy, he's wounded too!"

"We may need him, Frank. We may need every gun we've got before we get out of here. Now calm down and have somethin to eat."

Jake made sure that Frank was sitting down, and then he went over to check on Bill's wound. Luckily it was only a flesh wound that required little attention.

Wayne and John sat in utter amazement at what they had just seen. They could not believe that Frank would shoot one of his own group over something that small.

Frank sat there in silence trembling with rage. Slowly it dawned on him that what Jake had said made perfect sense. The redness left his face and he got up and put some wood on the fire. Then he walked toward where the horses were hobbled and reloaded his pistol, returning it to his belt when he was finished. Turning around, he came back to the fire and put the meat over the flames to roast. He straightened up and looked at each man. Slowly his gaze moved from one to the other.

To Bill, he said, "I'm right sorry for shootin ya like that. I guess I lost my head."

To Jake, he said, "thanks fer keepin' me from doin' somethin' I'd regret later."

To all of them, he said, "let's eat breakfast, and git on with our business."

To Frank, it was over and done with. It was in the past and soon to be forgotten. But to Bill, Wayne, and John, it was something to never be forgotten, and certainly never to be forgiven.

They knew that to stay with this man, meant that sooner or later, it would all boil down to either him or them.

After they had eaten breakfast, they all busied themselves with getting ready to move out. Bill and the two brothers, Wayne, and John, saddled their horses and removed the hobbles. As they were putting the bridles on, they kept a cautious eye on Frank and Jake, who were still seated at the campfire, talking in muffled tones.

Bill spoke to his friends in a hoarse whisper. "I don't know 'bout you boys, but I've had all I care to stomach of those two." It was obvious from the way he moved, that his arm was painful. He used only his right arm while putting the bit in his horse's mouth, and as he fastened the buckle on the bridle, having to engage both hands, he grimaced in pain.

Wayne and John both wagged their heads in agreement. "How do you propose we make the split from em, Bill? It ain't like they'll just up and let us go. They need our guns if'n they're goin' after that thar bear of a man we seen the tracks of," said Wayne. "Sides, I'd like to see what that coon has got for furs and such. He might even have him a squaw."

"I don't fancy havin' ta tell Frank and Jake thet we're leavin' right now," said John, his voice carrying farther than he had intended it to. A quick look in the

76

direction of the fire, confirmed that they were being watched, rather suspiciously. Hurriedly they finished with the horses and led them over to where Frank and Jake waited. They all tied their belongings to the backs of their saddles and mounted up.

Frank walked his horse a little out in front of the others and swung him around to face them. "You boys got somethin you want to complain about, now's yer time. We likely'll come up on this here trapper's camp in the next day or so. When we do, I want it understood that I call the shots. If 'n any of you got a problem with that, I want ta know it now."

They all looked around the circle at each other, but not a word was uttered, nor complaint made. They obviously still accepted Frank as leader and were not ready to make the break. They knew all too well that Jake and Frank, with the years of experience under their belts of living in these mountains, made it almost imperative they remain with them until Spring. That was only a couple of short months away. Maybe they could endure it that long. Right now, they faced a new adventure, and it was exciting for them to think of what they might find at this lone trappers camp. They thought of him as being alone because they were sure the other track they had seen belonged to a woman, and they were certainly not worried about any trouble a woman might give them. As a matter of fact, trouble from her only seemed to add to the excitement.

Frank reined his horse south on the trail that led so plainly through the snow. The rest of the group spurred their weary mounts to fall in behind him. Thoughts running through each of their heads of all the good things they might find before these next two days drew to a close.

Chapter Eleven

D al and Molly plodded steadily along, following the
path in the snow that was packed down from the
big trapper checking his traps on a regular basis. Dal
had his own thoughts as they headed for the farther
end of the line. He always started there and worked
his way back toward camp. He had a system and he
seldom varied from it, unless he suspected he was
being watched. At such times, he would never follow
a pattern, for that would make it too easy for someone
to lay in ambush for him. He saw no need today, however, of changing that pattern. To his knowledge, he and
Molly were the only ones around for miles, though the
smoke last night still disturbed him. He vowed silently
to himself that he would check on that when they got
back to camp. Meanwhile, he would keep a sharp eye
on their surroundings, just in case he was wrong. This
was second nature to him anyway. He rarely missed
anything that was different about his surroundings.

He recalled to himself how that one time, about
two years ago, he had been following an old game trail
through the mountains just Northwest of here. He was

hunting for his winter supply of meat as was necessary every year. He topped a small ridge, and his eyes caught a tannish brown spot in a thicket of spruce about twenty yards away. He had stopped immediately, letting his senses take over. Somehow, he had known that danger lurked in that thicket. It was almost like a sixth sense. His hair on his neck and arms seemed to always stand up straight, and his scalp prickled. This was one of those times, and he had learned to obey these feelings.

Slowly he had backed down the trail until he knew he wouldn't be visible from the other side of the ridge. He had then started in a wide circle that would eventually bring him to a point where he could see what was spooking him. With patience that few men have, he stalked the thicket. To anyone who might have been watching him, it would have been hard to see any movement at all. Yet he eventually made it to a spot that afforded him a view into that small clump of thickly branched evergreens. In its center, lay an Indian, with arrow knocked, waiting for him to step over the crest of that ridge.

Now Dal Trent had every reason to put a lead ball into this conniving redskin, and could have done so easily, but as he crouched here watching, he thought of something that seemed a whole lot more fun. Continuing with his slow stalk, he was able to get within ten feet of this brave, so intent was he at looking for Dal in the other direction. Dal had gathered himself to his full height, which was impressive at six feet seven inches, held his rifle in both hands at arm's length over his head, and let out the closest thing to a grizzly bear roar he could muster. The Indian had almost broken his neck as he swiveled his head around in Dal's direction. His eyes had almost popped from their sockets when he saw this huge apparition standing not over ten feet away! His feet and hands were digging and clawing to try and get him to a standing position. He had been so scared, that he had left his bow and arrows right there! Dal had laughed himself to tears then, and now as he recalled that poor Indian, he had to chuckle to himself.

They were nearing the end of the trap line, and the sun was still young in the sky. It was about midmorning, and Dal was pleased with their progress in reaching this point so soon. As they rounded the last bend in the trail, they could see the beaver dam that had flooded many acres of lowland. It was bordered by Aspen trees on two sides, and it was plain to see where the beavers were still active. Some of the trees were laying on the ground, where the beavers had been stripping it of the smaller branches and bark, and some of the trees still stood, but were girdled at the base where the beavers had used their sharp teeth to chip away at it, when eventually, they would fall, either during a windstorm, or after the little flat tails had successfully gnawed through it.

They stopped before they got to the edge of the pond and surveyed the area. Dal was of course familiar with it, but this was the first time Molly had seen this part of the valley. The sun was reflecting off the snow and the sky was perfectly blue. The softwood trees still held snow on their branches, and the hardwoods held a glimmering frost that sparkled like diamonds. The air was fresh and cold, and their breath created a vapor that hung in the air before their faces.

On the backside of the pond, directly opposite from where they were standing, the ground gently rose in elevation for about a half a mile. This was covered with a mixture of both hard and softwoods. Farther down toward the head of the dam, where one could see the dam itself, made up of sticks and mud the beavers had put together to successfully hold back this good-sized pond, the trees were sparser, until eventually it turned into open land with just a tree here and there. The side on which they stood was, for the most part barren of trees, except for those few Aspens that grew close to the waters' edge. Animal tracks dotted the snow and made their way toward the head of the dam. It was there the animals knew they could find water, and it was there the first of the traps were set.

"This is absolutely beautiful," Molly whispered. "I can see why you love this valley so much."

Dal turned his head and flashed a smile in her direction. "You know," he said, "I've never been anywhere that makes me feel more at home than here. This is where I'd like to finish out my days. Have you ever thought about what the future holds for you? Me, I guess I'm destined to be a trapper for the rest of my life."

"Well, there are worse things than being a trapper Dal," Molly whispered. "You could end up back in the settlements running a store or somethin'. I can't picture you wearing an apron, stocking shelves and waitin' on all the old ladies!"

Dal shot her a glance and had to grin as he too got a mental picture of himself trying to be nice to all the old busybodies who would come in for supplies. "I guess you're right, Molly. That would never work. I'm not really complainin' about my life out here. It's just that, well, it gets sort of lonely out here all alone. You know what I mean?"

"Yeah, I know what you mean, Dal. But it can get lonely even when you are with a whole lot of people too. The loneliest years of my life were when I was forced to live with the Indians." Molly slowly turned and took a couple of small steps away from Dal. She raised her eyes and allowed them to drink in all that surrounded her at this moment. Somehow, she just couldn't picture herself ever leaving this beauty and peacefulness that she was experiencing right now. She turned to face Dal, and as their eyes met, she just couldn't keep her mouth from saying, "we don t have to be lonely ever again, Dal." The words had barely left her mouth when a feeling of weakness came over her that bewildered and annoyed her at the same time. She hadn't meant to show the womanly side of herself to Dal. She had meant to keep up the strong front that she had learned so well while with the Indians who had loved her weak moments. It was during these times they had picked on her the hardest, hoping to break her to their will. Through the years of being held captive, she had learned to hide these weak moments. And so it was that she stood before this man she hardly knew, while feelings she had thought were no longer possible came over her. Her face reddened and she wished she could recall her words. It was a very awkward moment, and why was he just standing there anyway? Why didn't he say something?

Dal wasn't entirely sure that what he just heard was what he just heard! He was trying to cipher it all out in his own head when he noticed the look of embarrassment on her face. He shifted from one foot to the other and clearing his throat, he said what he hoped would ease this moment of awkwardness for them both. "I reckon we won't be lonely till Spring when you have to leave, and that's good. We've got a long day ahead of us, and I think we better get busy. I have to go along the shore of this dam to check my traps. The last one here is over near that little scrub pine, he said, gesturing to a scrawny little pine on the opposite side of where they now stood. It was probably about a half mile away. Do you want to stay here and watch, or do you want to come with me?"

"I want to come with you. That way I can see what you have to do with the traps, and the walking will help me stay warm." Molly could see that Dal was pleased as they turned their snowshoes toward the nearest trap. Dal cautioned Molly to not get too close to the edge of the water. "Sometimes, even though we've had freezing temperatures, there are spots that just don t freeze hard enough to support your weight. To get wet this time of year, means you might not make it to see Spring."

"Don t worry, I'll just follow you. I won't take any chances," Molly said.

"Speaking of taking chances," Dal said. "I'm still a might worried about that smoke I smelled yesterday. The tracks we left when I brought you into this valley haven t been totally covered with snow yet. I usually plan on getting my trapline pulled out there long before now for that very reason. I don't want any tracks leading down into this valley for any wandering eyes to see. If someone is out there who is bent on finding trouble, it would be all too easy to follow those tracks right to us. If I had got those traps pulled sooner, there wouldn't be any tracks leading straight to us now. Course, you wouldn't be here now if I had gone out earlier. No tellin' what would have happened to you if we hadn't met up. I guess what's happened is for the best. You just help me keep a sharp lookout while I've got my head down checking these traps. If trouble is goin' to come, I'd at least like a little warning!"

They were nearing the spot where the first trap was set, and they could see the snow was packed down in several directions leading to this one area. As they drew nearer, a mound of fur was visible off to the left of the trail next to a small group of Aspen. It was almost white in appearance, yet it was a different white than the snow. As they closed in on the animal, Molly could see the silvery tips on the fur, and she knew this was a silver fox. Dal had told her what they looked like, but she decided they were much more beautiful to see first-hand. The little creature raised its head and watched them approach. As they came within a few feet of the fox, it got to its feet and backed away from them as far as the chain on the trap would allow. When he came to the end, he faced them and growled out a warning to stay back. Dal took his pack off and dropped it at his feet. He withdrew his tomahawk and explained to Molly what was going to happen.

"I don't shoot any animals in my traps unless absolutely necessary. That way there are no holes in the pelts. I figure if the time ever comes when I can't look these little fellas in the eye that will be the time for me to quit. They deserve honesty just like anyone else".

"Dal, I don't see how you can trap those poor little animals. I...."

"Before you go any further," Dal interrupted, "let me explain something to you. These poor little animals, as you call them, if left totally alone, would over breed to the point of overrunning the entire area. Then they would develop diseases that would wipe them out. What few animals I take from this valley each year helps prevent this. And for the trapping part of it, the animals I take in these traps, are animals that you rarely see while out walking around, so it would be very difficult to shoot any of them. Trust me, trapping is the best way as long as the trap line is checked every day. I know there are those who oppose it, but there are those who oppose anything done in these mountains. Nobody knows until they've been here and lived like we are living right now."

"Dal, I didn't mean to suggest that it was wrong, I just don't think I could do what has to be done while they are looking me in the eye."

"It isn't easy at first. It's something you have to get past, and then it becomes automatic. Believe me, I have had times when it was difficult for me," Dal confessed. "You don't have to watch if you don t want to."

Dal walked toward the little fox, keeping his eyes fixed on the beady little black eyes. He kept the tomahawk slightly raised and off to one side, and when he was within arm's reach, with lightning speed the hawk slashed downward, and it was done. Without wasting any time, Dal freed the fox's' foot, and proceeded to reset the trap with a precision that comes with much experience. This done, he wiped the area clean of tracks with a pine bough. This would enable him to know on his next inspection what had gone on here just in case there was nothing in the trap.

Having done this, he turned and picked up the fox and attached it to his pack. After he had checked his traps and retrieved whatever they yielded, he would then find an area where he could skin the animals and dispose of the carcasses where they would not be smelled by anything that might be roaming in the area and henceforth scared away from the traps.

Molly was surprised by the efficiency Dal displayed in working the trap line. No move was wasted, and he was constantly alert to any danger that might be lurking close by. His eyes were constantly surveying the countryside, and it even seemed to her that he would take the time to sniff the air now and then. Watching him in this environment made him seem more animal than man. But she had seen enough of him to know that she was safe with him, and she felt that no matter what the circumstance, he would defend her to his death. She had never experienced those feelings before, but she knew she liked the way she felt. Here was a man she could be happy with, a man she would do anything for to make happy. All she had to do was make him see that!

Chapter Twelve

They continued around the trap line after eating a cold lunch of jerked beef and water and were nearing the last trap on the far side of the beaver dam, when Dal sensed trouble. He stopped midstride, and Molly almost ran into him. She started to say something to him about not stopping so suddenly, when he swiveled his head and placed his finger to his lips indicating for her to be quiet. She saw something was not right by the look on his face, and immediately her defenses were on guard.

They were stopped in front of a small clump of bushes that were about six feet high, so anyone looking at them from the East, would have a hard time distinguishing them from the bushes. The same held true from the West. Anyone looking at them from the North or South however, would be able to pick them out quite easily, as there was no cover in front or in back of them.

Dal knew this instantly, but to move would give away their location to anyone or anything that had not seen them yet. If they remained perfectly still, perhaps they would go undetected. Dal s and Molly s eyes were combing the countryside for movement or anything that seemed out of place. Off to their right, the trees were sparse, mostly hardwoods on slightly elevated ground, that allowed for a good field of view for about a mile. From that point, the terrain rose sharply to a sheer rock wall that was about seventy-five to one hundred feet high. There was no way in or out of this valley except by the trail Dal had used to bring Molly in. He was satisfied that the castle was hidden from view well enough so that unless someone walked right up to it, they would never see it.

Behind them was the beaver dam where they had just been. Dal felt certain the danger did not lie in that direction. Off to their left was more of the beaver dam, maybe fifty yards across. From that edge of the dam, the ground was pretty much the same as on this side, with maybe a few more trees scattered here and there. The danger, Dal concluded, must be from in front of them where the trees thickened, and visibility was low.

Having pinpointed, in his own mind where the danger lie, He decided that to stay still would only signal to whoever or whatever was posing the threat, that they had been detected. This whole process had taken only a few seconds and Dal now started forward at the same pace he had used before. In a muffled voice, he said to Molly, "keep yer eyes moving, but don t let on that you are suspicious at all. Maybe we can bluff our way out of this. If you see anything, tell me, but don't stop unless I do, understand?"

"Anything you say," Molly whispered. "Should I get my bow ready?"

"That would call too much attention. Just be ready to get it as fast as possible if the need arises, O.K.?"

"You got it," said Molly.

Slowly they made their way to the head of the beaver dam, where the trail would take them back to their left, or West. Dal was glad they would be heading back up the valley toward home. He was also glad the sun would be setting on their left and in the eyes of anyone who might be watching from the East. This would make it harder for anyone to track their movements except for those who might be close by.

Dal pondered what to do as he walked on and decided it would be wise not to go to the camp tonight. He would feel better having a wide-open space in which to be able to see anyone who might be trying to sneak up on them. Plus, if whoever was out there had not already discovered the castle, he didn't want to lead them to it now.

Just up ahead, was a small group of spruce trees that would give some shelter from the cold, and also help to hide them from prying eyes. As they neared it, Dal explained to Molly what they were going to do. She nodded in agreement, and they set about digging out the snow for a campfire and place of shelter. Soon, they were sitting on their packs around a warm fire, eating venison steaks they had brought with them, as the sun slowly sank to the bottom of the sky and disappeared. With the disappearance of the sun, came the chill of the evening that penetrated to the very core. Both Dal and Molly were thankful for the warmth of the fire, and they huddled close together, as close to the fire as they dared. Before long, a steak sizzled, as juices dripped in the flames. Molly added snow to their coffee pot and soon it was boiling, ready for the coffee to be added. As they enjoyed the meal and each other's company, their bodies relaxed and the heat from the fire made them drowsy. Darkness stole around them, and only what was illuminated by the firelight was visible to them. The moon, full on this night, began its ascent through the canopy of stars that winked at them from all four points of the compass. Somewhere in the distance a lone wolf was heard, as he poured out his soul to the moon. Trees were popping as the cold penetrated and froze them. For Dal and Molly, right here, right now, was the best a man or a woman could ask for. This was what living in the wilderness was all about. Nothing else even came close to the feelings generated by nights like this. Somehow even the fact that danger might be lurking in the darkness somewhere out there, seemed to add to this feeling. If asked to explain it, they probably would not even find the words. But the feelings were definitely there. There were other feelings present here tonight also. Feelings they had both tried to suppress in the past few weeks. They both knew these thoughts would have to be dealt with at a later date, but not tonight, not now. There were other things more important right now, like staying alive for the next few `hours. Each of them knew they were going to have to deal with the ever-growing feelings, but tonight was not the night.

They both understood these feelings would have to be dealt with sooner or later. These feelings of what? What were these feelings? Love, that is what it had to be. None of these feelings had ever been felt by either of them before. Dal's mind raced back to the day he had met her, and he thought to himself how he hadn't had a clue that Molly could be anything other than a poor captive woman. He really had not planned on ever finding one who he could be happy with. That had been the farthest thing from his mind. Everything had been going just as planned with his life. More furs than he could possibly need, that would bring more money than he could possibly spend on the meager supplies needed for the life of a mountain man. Beauty surrounded him on every side. Everywhere he looked, he saw the handiwork of God here in this wilderness and he had never planned on going back to civilization. Since his first day here, he had known this was the place for him. But now, well, beauty of a different kind was seated on the other side of this campfire. Beauty that in some ways outshone the natural beauty of the mountains. But this beauty was, no doubt, going to complicate his life in a way he had never seen, and he wasn't sure how he was going to handle it.

Molly sat on the opposite side of the fire staring into the darkness, lost in her own thoughts. She also thought of the day when Dal and she had met. When she finally realized he posed no threat to her, what a relief for her to know she did not have to face the hardships of living in these mountains alone anymore. She too, had not in her wildest dreams thought that she would ever find a man here in this vast wilderness who would be anyone she might be happy with. But there sat the most handsome, kind, gentle man she had ever met. Yes, she could imagine spending the rest of her life with him, whether it was here in the High Lonesome or back in the settlements. She knew that if Dal ever got around to asking her, she would say yes in a heartbeat. However, as it stood right now, she wasn't at all sure how Dal felt about her. Yes, he had shown some feelings toward her that could be interpreted as positive, but she didn't dare to get her hopes too high. She would let Dal make the first move, then she would know how he felt. She couldn't bear the thought of being rejected. Better to play it safe and then if he never said or did anything to pursue her, she at least would not have made a fool out of herself. How awkward would that be?

Right now, they faced uncertainty of what this night would bring. They knew not what danger lurked out there in the darkness, and how it would present itself to them. She and Dal both had no doubts concerning their abilities to defend themselves in any given situation, but not knowing who or what was out there was a little unnerving to Molly. Dal, however, took things as they came, and rarely allowed himself to get nervous about anything. This was due in part to his easygoing personality, but he also had learned through his years in the mountains, to face things as they came. Sometimes things came at you so fast, there was no time to think or worry over the outcome. It all came down to, you either lived or you died. The trail ended or it stretched out before you.

And so it was, that while they were both lost in thoughts of their own, the night continued to wear on. Dal was the first to notice the change in the air and he mentioned it to Molly. "It's goin' to snow," Dal said. It was then that Molly too felt the change. "I think you're right, Dal," Molly replied. "I can feel the moisture in the air."

Dal seemed to be lost in thought and didn't reply. Molly watched him but didn't speak again. A lone wolf howled in the distance, and the clouds continued to thicken and cover the moon. She could see the clouds swirl as the wind toyed with them. She watched the moon disappear behind the bank of dark, snow laden clouds, and wondered how much snow they would drop on them before morning. It was a good thing they had their snowshoes with them, she reflected. Otherwise, they could become stranded in waist deep snow. She had seen many a storm that could swallow a man. Nature played no favorites out here.

"I've got a plan," Dal stated, matter of factly. "When it starts to snow, we're gonna make our move. We'll gradually put a good amount of wood on the fire, so it will last. That way if we are being watched like I think we are, they won't notice any change until we have gotten a good start. I'm calculating' on a sizable snowfall, and if that happens, it will hide our trail, and they won't know which way we went. I'm bettin' whoever it is out there, if there's more'n one, they will have a sentry watching the glow of our fire. As cold as it is, they need a fire also, but they'll keep it back so we can't see it. That means they'll have to change sentries often, so they don't freeze to death. I'm a hopin' what with all that commotion, they won't notice any difference in our fire 'til we're long gone. Once we're away from here, I'll decide what the best course of action will be for us to take. I'm gonna need to find out how many of them there are. That way we'll know what we're up against. This I know, they're not Injuns, 'cause Injuns wouldn't be out in this weather. They have sense enough to stay put. These coons are either dumb or desperate!"

Chapter Thirteen

Quite some distance from Dal and Molly's camp, Frank, Jake, Wayne, and Bill were seated around their campfire trying to stay warm. John was at a vantage point where he could see the glow from their intended victim's fire. This, he thought, was boring and extremely cold work. He would be glad to get back to the warmth of the fire. He wasn't sure why Frank had insisted on posting a sentry. These people weren't going anywhere at night. Who would leave the comfort of the fire when it was this cold? He was glad he only had a few more minutes on his watch and waited impatiently for one of the others to relieve him. The cold was really beginning to seep into his bones, and he tried to move around a little to keep his blood circulating. He heard a wolf and shuddered at the mournful sound. He hoped that wolf stayed away. Many a story had been told around the campfire about hungry wolves coming into a camp at nighttime and making a meal of the poor unsuspecting inhabitant.

Time pushed slowly onward and finally he heard footsteps approaching from the direction of his camp.

He turned to see who it was that was to relieve him and was surprised to see Frank approaching. "Go on back to the fire, John," Frank said as he came up to him. "Ya don't have to tell me twice, Frank," returned John. "I thought I was gonna freeze to death out here. How's come you came back out, I thought it was Bill's turn?"

"It was, but I figured him bein' so skittish and all, I'd let him come out later when them down yonder will be sleepin'. You git on back to the fire and warm up 'cause I'll prob'ly need ya to come back out later," said Frank.

John turned and headed back to the camp anticipating the warmth of the fire and some hot food in his belly. Their camp was situated quite some distance from where he had been keeping watch. It was located behind the only rock formation in this particular area that was large enough to conceal the glow from the fire that was now welcoming John back to its warmth.

Frank settled down for his watch and shivered as the cold, night air began to penetrate his clothing. He noticed an apparent change in the air and looked skyward to watch the clouds swirl and play around the moon before finally darkening it out completely. He could hardly see his hand in front of his face, now the light from the moon was gone. It was feeling like snow he decided. That would be good for he felt that would keep those down yonder holed up 'til it was done. He felt confident that by this time tomorrow, his little band of thieves would be dividing the plunder among themselves. They might have to torture them to get them to tell where their main camp was at, but Frank was good at that. He even took pride in his work.

He always had enjoyed watching pain work its wiles on a victim. They always vowed they would never tell him what he wanted to know, but in time, they always talked.

The four men huddled around the fire as close as they dared get without setting their fur coats on fire, and yet the cold was always pressing in on them from the outside of the circle. Only one side could be warmed at a time, and when that side was warmed, the other three sides were cold. Because of this, they had to keep turning almost constantly to stay warm.

Finally, Jake said to the others, "I think it's time we break out the bedrolls, boys. We'll stay lots warmer inside them."

"You don't have to tell me twice," returned Bill, as he strode to his horse and untied his bedroll from the back of the saddle.

The lone wolf that had been howling all evening, started in once more, closer now it seemed. The forms around the campfire craned their necks to try and locate the direction from which the sound came, but the wind made it seem like it came from everywhere.

Bill quickly unrolled his bedroll and crawled inside. His eyes were large, and he wished he were anywhere but here.

"Hey, Bill," Jake spoke across the fire. "Don't forgit, Frank wants ya to relieve him in about an hour, so don't git too comfy in them thar robes."

Bill grunted but didn't say a word as he snuggled deeper. He thought to himself how he wished this night was over. He wasn't sure he could stand that time when he would have to spell Frank, the cold, the time alone, and with that wolf out there somewhere. He didn't know why they didn't just go on down there and kill whoever was down there and get it done with. Why all this when there were five of them and only one man and a squaw out there. It just didn't make any sense to him. It seemed like Frank enjoyed playing cat and mouse with his prey. These thoughts flooded his mind as he drifted off to sleep in the relative comfort of his robes.

Jake, John, and Wayne joined Bill one by one as they each climbed into their respective bedroll. Soon loud snores were heard from all sides of the fire, while overhead, snowflakes began drifting to earth, slowly at first, and then with more intensity, until the air was full. The storm was upon them.

Chapter Fourteen

About a mile away, Dal and Molly were also wrapped in robes around their campfire. As soon as Dal felt the first snowflake, he turned his head to Molly who was sound asleep, and said in a hushed whisper, "Molly, wake up." Instantly her eyes were open and focused on Dal's face.

"What is it, Dal?" she asked.

"We have to get our stuff together. It's beginning to snow. I want our tracks to be totally obliterated by this storm, so our guests won't know which way we went. I'm not sure yet what our course of action is going to be, but I don't want them knowing where we are. We'll at least have that much in our favor." Dal said. "We better get our snowshoes on." With that, they both set about fastening their snowshoes to their boots.

Molly slowly got to her feet and shouldered her pack, along with her quiver full of arrows. Her bow she kept in her hand where it could be easily brought into use if the need arose. "Do you think they can see us when we leave?" Molly asked, sounding a little worried.

"No worries there, Molly," Dal replied. "With this snow coming down as hard as it is, they'll be lucky to see twenty paces ahead of 'em. No need to bother with the fire anymore either, 'cause I'm sure they can't see it anymore. We'll just let it die out on its' own. You just follow me, Molly, and we'll skedaddle on out of here!"

With that, he shouldered his own pack which weighed close to a hundred pounds, what with the normal supplies he usually carried and the furs he had collected along the way up to this point. He wished they could have finished checking the entire trapline. Had it not been for this little unexpected turn of events they would have been on their way back to their main camp about midday tomorrow. As he turned that thought around in his head, he began to think that might be the best course of action after all. There would be no way they would be able to be tracked the way the snow was falling now. And besides, he didn't want he and Molly to be caught so far away from the main camp with so much snow that was sure to fall tonight. If they pushed themselves, they could be back at the castle before dawn. That way Molly would be safe in the practically impenetrable shelter, and he could deal with these guys on his own terms. With his mind made up, he turned to Molly. "We're headed for the castle. Are you up for a little hike tonight?"

"You just lead, Dal, and I'll follow. I reckon I can keep up, so you just go ahead and set the pace," Molly said as she flashed him a smile.

"You asked for it," Dal shot back at her with a smile of his own. Without another word, he plunged into the darkness and vanished from her sight. Immediately she knew she would have to stay right on the tail of his snowshoes to keep from being separated from him. That would mean disaster, so with all her might, she pushed herself into the night following the man she trusted her life to.

Dal seemed to have an uncanny ability to find his way from one point to another, regardless of what lay between those two points. Tonight, was no different. Even though the snow continued to fall so heavily it was impossible to see more than an arm's length ahead of them, the course he set was true. They encountered no other obstacle as they trudged through the snowy darkness, and just before dawn, they were standing in sight of the castle. Under any other circumstances, Dal would have gone directly to his fortress, glad to be home from his trapline. This time, however, he was taking no chances.

He spoke to Molly as he came to a halt. "I reckon we should play it safe, Molly. Instead of just walking right in, I want to be sure we're not bein' watched. You stay put right here, whilst I trek on up to a vantage point just off to the left of the castle. It won't take me very long, and I'll be back in no time a' tall."

"You really think they could have followed us through this storm Dal?" Molly asked.

"No, I don't think they could, but I just want to be sure," Dal replied. "You can make your way very slowly in the direction of our shelter, just don't go in till I get back, O.K.?"

"O.K.," Molly agreed.

Dal started off in the direction of a tall formation of rock that stood at least fifty feet higher than any other spot around. Once on top, he knew it would command a view of the entire area. The snow was stopping and there were breaks in the clouds, with blue sky showing through from time to time as the clouds drifted lazily toward the East. He knew instinctively that cold air would be moving in from the North, and he longed to be holed up in the comfort and warmth of the castle.

He wondered as he walked along when he had started referring to the shelter that had been hewn out of the canyon wall, as "the castle." It just seemed to be the proper name for it. He recalled reading about castles across the sea in Scotland, Ireland, and England, when in school back in the settlement, and how they were practically impenetrable by the enemy, easily defended, and seldom conquered. This shelter was, indeed, all of that and more. Dal knew that with the store of lead and powder he had, he could hold off a large war party with ease. There was only one way for an enemy to attack and that was completely in the open. No one could get within rifle range without being detected. The face of the canyon wall that made up the front of the castle, was not recognizable as anything other than a canyon wall from any distance. It was because of these facts Dal was not particularly concerned that whoever was out there would have seen the castle on their way into the canyon.

When he reached the spot where he would begin his ascent to the top of the rock formation, he took off his snowshoes and stood them up in the snow. The climb to the top was not a difficult one, though it was slippery with the new fallen snow, and soon he was lying on his belly, peering into the valley below. The view that lay before him never ceased to amaze him with its beauty. The sun was just now beginning to crest the canyon rim, and it cast its golden fingers of light across the entire landscape. The snow that had just fallen last night, lay in feet upon the ground, and covered all with a fresh new blanket of pure white. Diamonds glimmered and shone in the sunlight as far as the eye could see. Even on the branches of the trees, the snow was thick and heavy, bowing them toward the ground. Now and then, a loud pop could be heard as a pine branch gave up under the weight of the snow and toppled to the ground beneath.

Dal focused his scrutiny starting from his left to his right. He would fasten his gaze on one object and hold on it for several seconds. If anything was moving out there, his peripheral vision would pick it up. He continued his surveillance this way until he had covered the entire valley floor and was satisfied that nothing was moving that shouldn't be.

He retraced his steps to the bottom where his snowshoes waited for him, strapped them on, and started his way back to Molly. He now knew it was safe to make their way to the security of the home he had come to love. Within a few short minutes, he was at Molly's side.

"Well?" Molly asked.

"It's safe for now," said Dal. "Instead of going straight to the door of the castle, we'll make a long sweeping circle, and stay close to the canyon wall as we get to the door. That way there won't be a visible path leading to our front door. I wish we had gotten here while it was still snowing, so our tracks were covered, but we'll just have to do it this way and hope for the best."

"You know, Dal," Molly started. "I think I may have been with the Indians a little too long."

"Well, I would think that any time spent with them would be too much," Dal replied, "but why do you say that?"

"I was thinking while you were up looking over the valley, and even though we may be in danger, and don't even know what kind of danger yet, it's all kind of exciting!"

"I'll remember that if that danger ever gets here," teased Dal. "You can be the first in line to deal with it, since it excites ya and all!"

"I reckon I could handle it if it comes to that," Molly retorted. "You ain't dealin' with one of them gals from the settlements who only knows how to clean an' cook. This bow is deadly out to fifty yards or more, and I know how to use it. Just let someone try to get in here and they'll find out they're dealin' with a wildcat!"

"I'm glad I'm on this side of that bow. I think it's the safest place to be," said Dal. "Let's get on up to the castle and start a fire. I'm 'bout starving, and I'm thinking a little heat would feel good right about now. It's beginning to get colder, and I've got a feelin' that it's gonna be one of the coldest nights yet this winter."

As they neared the entrance to their snug little fortress, they took care to stay as close to the canyon wall as possible, so as not to leave any visible tracks leading straight to the door. Dal stopped and looked at the snowshoe trail behind them and was satisfied they could not have done better. He stepped to the door and took off his snowshoes, as did Molly also, and then he used one of the snowshoes like a shovel and scooped the snow from in front of the door, so they wouldn't carry any unnecessary snow inside with them as they opened the door and stepped inside.

Everything was exactly the same as they had left it, and they both set about doing what needed to be done to get a fire going and some food cooking. Dal lit the wood that was already arranged in preparation for a fire.

"Why do you always have a fire ready to go before you even leave?" Molly wondered.

"Well, it's like this," Dal began. "A couple of years ago, I was out running my trapline and I made a misstep and ended up in the water up to my neck. Before I got back to my camp, I was about froze to death. When I finally did make it back, I had to fumble around with wood and tinder to get a fire going. I vowed I would never have to do that again. So, if I leave a fire going when I go out for a day or two, and can't arrange the wood, then I at least make sure that all I will need to get a fire going in a matter of minutes is close at hand."

"One thing I've noticed about being out here, and that is that experience is a great teacher," reflected Molly.

"It is if it don't kill ya first," said Dal. "Some folks just don't learn very easy. Them are the ones who usually don't make it back."

Molly had gotten a large piece of elk meat from the storage room and had it spitted over the fire. The juices began to sizzle and crackle as they dripped into the fire, and the delicious aroma filled the room, making their mouths water with hunger. She went outside and dipped the coffeepot into the snow and came back in and placed the pot over the fire so the snow would melt. When that was accomplished, she put in the ground coffee and set the pot on to boil. They both were beginning to anticipate how the hot coffee was going to taste along with the juicy elk meat, and they both sat around the fire and watched with interest until the meal was ready to enjoy. Dal then took his prized knife that his father had given to him, it seemed like decades ago, and carved a piece of meat for each of them, while Molly poured them steaming cups of coffee. Then, they each settled back in their chair and began to eat in silence, each of them lost in their own thoughts.

Today would be a day of keeping close watch down the valley to see if their uninvited company would show themselves. Dal doubted if they would, but he couldn't be sure. He figured they would probably show up sometime during the night to try and surprise them. The surprise, however, would not be on he and Molly. He had a plan that he had been fabricating in his mind all night as they had snowshoed back to the castle. Soon he would share this plan with Molly and the part he wanted her to play in it, and then they could set about getting ready for what, he was sure, would be a long night ahead.

As they finished their meal, they both were over-come with weariness, and so they each took their place, Molly on the bed, and Dal on the floor, to take a much-needed rest. Soon they were each snoring away, fast asleep, oblivious to the world around them.

The sun outside was about halfway to its zenith, and the newly fallen snow was blinding to the naked eye. Anyone spending much time in that brightness, could be blinded in a very short time, if precautions were not taken. Dal and Molly would not have to worry about that, for they would sleep for the better part of the day, knowing that night could bring an enemy, unseen as of yet, down on them.

The day wore on with the sun reaching its zenith, and then starting down the back slant of its journey. Just before It slipped below the western horizon, Dal was awake and scanning the valley through one of the two windows in the front of the castle. Each of these windows consisted of thick planking held together with rawhide thongs soaked in water and then allowed to dry after being wrapped around each plank several times, thus holding the plank firmly together. Each window had four such planks, two on each side, with leather hinges which allowed them to be swung back out of the way, either to allow cooler air to enter in the summer, or to allow the inside occupants the ability to shoot freely in any direction. When closed, anyone from the outside looking at the wall could not tell that they were even there, unless within a few feet of the wall itself.

Satisfied there was no movement down the valley, Dal closed the window, and lashed it securely in place with a rawhide thong. He realized as he turned his attention to the inside, that he was feeling hungry once again. Molly seemed to still be sleeping so he decided he would stoke the fire and place more meat on the spit to roast. He moved about with the ease, silence, and grace of a man whose life had depended on such movement many times before. Soon the fire was licking hungrily at the wood, and the meat was giving off a mouthwatering aroma that woke Molly from her slumber. She stretched and sat up in bed grinning at Dal who now sat in a chair at the table. He grinned back at her and said, "I thought you jes' might sleep right on through the night, the way you was snorin'! You sounded about like an ol' grizzly bar' that was holed up fer the winter!"

Her eyes snapped as she retorted in obvious good nature, "you should have laid awake and listened to yourself it you think I was snoring'. I didn't think I was goin' to get any sleep at all the way you started in snoring'. That's the reason I had to sleep longer than you, so I could get the same amount of sleep as you!" She laughed as she slid her legs down over the edge of the bed and dropped to the floor, heading toward Dal, who feigned a look of disbelief at what she had just said. She intended to slap him on the shoulder, but as she tried, his hand suddenly reached out and caught hers. She yelped in surprise at the speed he had just displayed, and he spun her around and caught her on his lap as she lost her footing. His arms encircled her waist and held her in a bearlike hug. She was taken with such surprise that she turned her face toward his to reprimand him for such actions. Their eyes met and for an instant, held on each other. Then the moment was over, and they quickly regained their composure. She, laughing, and playfully slapping him again on the shoulder, and he, very embarrassed, dropped his arms and allowed her to get up from his lap. A few minutes of awkward silence passed, and then everything was back to normal, or so it seemed. Dal, however, was shaken to the core. He had not intended to allow this to happen. But now that it had, he seemed to want more of it. He suddenly realized that this woman, whose life he had saved simply by being in the right spot at the right time, was the one he would spend the rest of his life with. He didn't know if she realized it or not, but that didn't matter. She was the one for him, and he knew it.

Chapter Fifteen

Soon after Dal and Molly left the campfire the night before, Frank had waited for Bill to relieve him. He had left strict instructions that he wanted to be relieved in one hour. It had been closer to three now Frank estimated, and his patience was about worn out. He was cold, and the snow was coming down so hard he couldn't see anything. Slowly he rose to his feet, as he allowed his muscles to stretch. He noticed more and more lately that if he didn't remain active, his muscles tightened up and it was hard for him to move as freely as he used to.

He turned in the direction of his camp, and started off slowly at first, then faster as his body loosened up. Soon he was standing over a dying fire, where three forms huddled in their bedrolls under fur blankets, snores resounding from all four. They were totally oblivious to anything going on around them, and had Frank been an enemy, they would all have been dead. As a matter of fact, Frank was so mad right now, he thought about killing them himself.

He stooped and grabbed a large piece of wood and tossed it into the dying embers. Flames came to life almost immediately as they caught on the bone-dry wood. He retrieved one more piece and added that also. Within seconds the flames were three feet high, and heat was emanating from the fire. Frank took his rifle and jabbed each of the prone forms, not very gently either. All three came too with a start and rubbed their eyes as the brightness of the fire temporarily blinded them. They soon became aware of Frank standing over them with his rifle pointed menacingly in their direction. They, all three, sat up slowly as they continued to stare into the muzzle of that .50 caliber rifle. They had all seen Frank mad before and they knew the look on his face right now was not one of joy. They also knew that Frank tended to lose all reason when he was mad, so they were not at all positive what his intentions were at this point. They all knew he only had one shot from that gun, but none of them wanted to be the unlucky recipient of that bullet. It was a tense few minutes without a word exchanged, until Frank seemed to regain some sense of normalcy and lowered the barrel of the rifle to the ground.

"What in tarnation do you boys think you're doin'?" Frank asked, as he spat a stream of tobacco juice into the fire. "If'n I'd been a band of Injuns, yer scalps'd be hangin' from some bucks' belt right now."

"Sorry, Frank, we wasn't thinking," said Jake. "We was tired as all tarnation, and that fire just put us to sleep. I know we should've posted a lookout. It won't happen again."

Frank always seemed to accept what Jake said, and this time was no different. He looked each of them in the eye, and with a shrug of his shoulders, let the matter drop. "We have to get movin' at first light," Frank began. "Let's hope they were as sleepy as you coons were last night. Maybe, just maybe, we'll catch them off guard. With all this new snow, we can sneak up without being heard if'n we do it right. You boys check yur rifles and make sure the powder is dry. We'll split up and come at them from all sides. That way there will be no way either of them can get away. That thar bear of a man, you can shoot to kill if you have to, but that squaw, I'd like to keep alive. I think she might come in handy later on," Frank added with a wink and grin.

The others caught his meaning and grins were flashed around the fire as they each had his own thoughts about what he would do with that squaw.

"How you planning on splittin' us up, Frank?" asked John.

"I figure we'd split up five ways and come at 'em from five different directions. The only thing we have to be careful of is getting caught in the crossfire. Once we see 'em, adjust your position so you ain't shooting at each other," said Frank.

Bill shifted uncomfortably and it was easy to see he was not pleased with the arrangement Frank had just laid out for them. Had he not been petrified of Frank, he would have left the group right then. He was jittery and scared of being on his own to come at the camp. His mind raced and he could see all kinds of bad things happening, including himself getting shot. And then there was that wolf they kept hearing all night long. Where was he right now? Were there more than just one out there, just waiting for a chance to dash in and kill him? His nerves were frayed and almost at the breaking point. But all these things he would not say out loud, because Frank would be very upset. Instead, he busied himself checking his rifle and powder.

Wayne and John didn't seem to be bothered by the plan, and Jake of course, thought anything Frank came up with was great.

Frank began to lay out the plan in more detail to the four men gathered around the fire as the first gray streaks of dawn began to show in the Eastern sky. Ever so slowly, red began to mix with the gray, as the sun began its ascent. "Everybody listen closely, 'cause I'm only goin' to say this once. We'll begin by making a big circle, and we'll drop a man off every few hundred yards, startin' with you Bill, then John, Wayne, Jake, and then me. We have to move fast so this can all happen under cover of darkness. As soon as I'm in position, I'll call like an owl, and we'll start movin' in. It's a simple plan but it'll work. Any questions?"

No questions were voiced, so they followed Frank away from the fire. They would retrieve their horses after this was all done. Each man carried only the essential items needed to get the job done, knife, rifle, powder, and lead.

The snow was thigh deep as they made their way toward the camp, circling wide to avoid detection. Frank told Bill when to drop off from the group, and soon they were gone from his sight. They proceeded as planned until they were in a complete circle around the targeted camp. As Frank got into position, he gave his owl hoot, and then slowly crept forward. As soon as the others heard the owl call, they all started closing in.

As fate would have it, Frank was the first to reach the camp of the intended mischief and saw that it was empty. Dawn was now at hand and visibility was getting better every minute. Frank could see the others as dark specks on the white background of the newly fallen snow. He looked around the deserted campsite and noticed there were no tracks that could be seen that would reveal the direction their intended victims had taken. He leaned down to try and find some indentation in the snow where their tracks exited from the fire they had enjoyed here in this little spot. Nothing was visible, so he stood back up to see the progress the others were making. The way he was positioned, put Bill at his back and to his left. The others were all in a circle around Frank.

Bill had begun to freak out the moment he could no longer see the others. It just got worse as time went on until when he saw Frank stand up, he knew in his own mind that this had to be the man they had planned to kill. His eyes went wide, and his breath came in short gasps, as he raised his rifle and pointed it at the man. As soon as the sights lined up on his target, he pulled the trigger.

The .50 caliber ball caught Frank in the middle of the back and tore out the front of his chest. He was dead before he hit the ground.

Bill began to shout for joy, "I got 'im, I got 'im! Frank, did ya see that? I got 'im!"

The others weren't at all sure what had happened, so they were a little reluctant to hurry until they knew for sure that the big man they had planned on killing was actually dead. Bill on the other hand, sure he had killed the right man, and eager to hear Frank's words of praise, ran as fast as he could in the deep snow.

As Bill neared the corpse, he knew in a heartbeat what he had done. How could he have mistaken Frank for the giant they were after? He slowly let his rifle slip from his grasp, and he sank into the snow, sobbing and saying over and over, "I'm sorry Frank, I'm sorry Frank. I didn't know it was you."

As the other three neared the scene, they also knew what had happened. They could only stare incredulously at the figure that was once their leader, and at Bill as he continued to ramble. The seriousness of the matter and what they were now facing began to dawn on each of them, except Bill. He seemed to have lost all sanity.

It was Jake who spoke first. "We have to decide now what we are goin' to do. Are we going to pursue our original plan or give it up and git out of this part of the country?"

"How in tarnation are we going to know which direction they went?" asked Wayne. "Their tracks are completely covered up. It don't even look like they was here at all last night."

"They must've cleared out at fust sign of snow." offered John.

"What are we gonna do with Frank?" queried Bill.

"Nothin' we can do with him, unless'n you want to dig a grave," said Jake. "We'll just have to leave him here. The wolves and ravens will take right nice care of 'im. All that will be left of him will be bones come Spring. We'll just take his gun and everythin' else he won't be needin', and head on out of this valley, 'lessn you want to finish what we come in here fur."

"I'm all for gittin' out while the gittin's good," said Bill trying not to look in the direction where Frank lay. "I've had 'nough of these here mountains to last me a lifetime. I should've gone when I wanted to, and Frank would still be alive. I jist cain't believe I shot one of my own partners."

"I say we stay and get revenge on this here giant and his squaw for Frank," Jake said. "He was leadin' us and that was what we was a 'gonna do when he was alive. I vote we stay and see this through to the end. I'm takin' over the leadership of this little band, since I'm next in line after Frank. Anybody got any objections?"

The other three men looked at Jake and then at each other. Wayne stomped his feet in an attempt to get the blood circulating once again, then as he turned to face Jake, he said, "I reckon you'll do OK by us Jake, just so long as you don't lose your temper like Frank used t 'do. I don't think I could put up with that anymore."

John grunted his agreement and said, "I'll put in with ya Jake, just so long as you aren't like Frank used to be. I'm all for seein what this giant has got for furs. Maybe he's even got some gold. We know for sure he's got him a squaw. That's almost as good as gold! You got any idee 'bout how we kin find em?"

122

"I'll have to think on that fer a spell, but they cain't be too far away. Why don't you boys take what Frank won't be needin anymore, and I'll see if'n I can spot any signs around here to pint us in the right di-rection." Jake turned and started to make a sweep of the area around where Dal and Molly had spent part of the night before, in search of any clue that would point them to where they had so mysteriously disappeared. Jake wasn't sure why they had seen no sign of a winter camp when they came into this valley, but he knew there had to be one somewhere. No one could survive a whole winter without some shelter, and he knew from the evidence he had already seen of this man, that he was the kind of man who did not leave anything to chance. He must have been aware of their presence last night otherwise he wouldn't have left the warmth of his fire to head off in a blizzard on foot. This fact spoke volumes to Jake, who had as much mountain experience as Frank had, and really had more common sense than Frank had had. He knew instinctively that if it came to a fight with this, as yet unseen man, it would be a fight not soon forgotten. This man they were about to pursue, was a true mountain man, who probably thought more like an Indian or wild animal than a white man. He would have to be dealt with very carefully, if they expected to come out of it alive.

Therefore, it was that Jake decided they would proceed with caution and stealth. They had all the time in the world to locate his camp, and he felt confident they could scout it out without detection and decide the best course of action. He knew he would have to keep an eye on Bill who, he felt, was about ready to lose his sanity. The success of this whole plan depended on how Bill reacted to everything from now on. If it came right down to it, he just might have to put a bullet or knife in him to keep him quiet. That would be unfortunate because they needed every man they had. He'd just have to cross that bridge when he came to it. Right now, they had to determine which direction they needed to take.

The sun was now directly in his face which made it nearly impossible to see anything, so he made his way back to where the other three men were just finishing up stripping Frank of anything valuable.

"Cover him up with snow and let's get away from here," Jake said.

"Did you find any sign of 'em?" asked Bill.

"Not one thing that would show me where they headed," Jake replied. "But I'll tell you what we're gonna do. We're gonna split up, so's we can cover more ground. We'll each take a different di-rection and meet back here before sunset."

"Now you jest hold on a minute thar Jake," cried Bill. "Thar ain't no way I'm goin' off by myself, not after what jest happened here. I jest don't do well on my own."

"He's got a point thar, Jake," exclaimed John.

Wayne spoke up and said, "why don't we jest go out in pairs? John and me can go together and you and Bill can go in a different di-rection. Thet way, we'll have four sets of eyes instead of two. What do ya say Jake?"

After a minute of thought, Jake spoke up. "I guess thet would work. We'll still meet back here before sun-down. And don't git caught in the dark. If'n ya do, yer on yer own."

And so, they departed in different directions, each satisfied they could handle any situation that might arise, and each filled with confidence of the abilities they possessed. Each that is, except Bill. He was skit-tish and full of trepidation about what might lie ahead. As Jake led the way, he followed close on his heels, not willing they should become separated.

Jake set a course that would take them back toward the entrance to the valley, which was West, and John and Wayne headed in a Southerly direction. The snow was nearly to their thighs and walking was very slow. They didn't have any snowshoes and they had decided to give their horses a rest by leaving them behind. They knew they would not wander far in the deep snow, and they would be busying themselves with foraging for whatever grasses they could uncover. Each man carried a small pack with leftover meat and their bedrolls, plus their guns and powder, lead, and knives. They were traveling light and despite their lack of experience, they were all in good physical shape., so they made good time. The sun was making its way up the sky and Jake estimated it to be about midmorning. They should have plenty of time to scout out two or three miles with what daylight they had left, and still have plenty of time to make it back to their rendezvous point before darkness settled over the valley.

John and Wayne split up as soon as they started out and were soon about two hundred yards apart, each moving at the same pace and heading in the same direction. This gave them a good view of what was ahead of them and increased their chances of spotting something. The going was very difficult and the trek through the deep snow sapped their strength. Their thighs burned with exertion they were putting forth, and their breaths came in rapid succession, the frigid air threatening to freeze their lungs. Instinctively, they slowed their pace even more, but continued to keep a sharp eye for whatever might be moving, or just might look out of place.

Jake had to force Bill to split up from him, and felt he had to keep his eye on him more than on the countryside around him. Soon, however, it seemed that

Bill settled down and got the hang of it. He kept pace with Jake and appeared to be keeping a sharp lookout. Satisfied that at last Bill was coming into it, Jake was able to himself, keep alert to his surroundings.

The valley was different somehow, now there were more beings present here. The birds were quieter. The animals kept hidden, and overall, it was just different.

Chapter Sixteen

Dal sensed there was something different about this morning in the air. If asked, he wouldn't have been able to tell you what was different about it, but it was just a feeling. Something in his subconscious that told him, "the valley is different this morning." With this feeling, came a foreboding that something was going to happen. And with this foreboding, came an alertness that only being in the mountains alone for five or six years can produce. He was in his element, and there was no equal, be it Indian or mountain man.

He had been waiting for this to happen, as he knew it would. These men were intent on causing he and Molly harm, of this, he was sure. Otherwise, they would have openly approached their camp last night instead of keeping lookout from a distance. He had no doubt they were enemies. He knew what he must do.

Molly sensed the change in him almost immediately, and asked him as he stood looking down the valley from the window inside the castle, "what's wrong Dal?"

"There's something brewing in the valley, Molly. I feel it in my bones. Don't ask me how I know. It's just a feeling I get before something happens. It hasn't failed me yet."

"What are we gonna do?" asked Molly

"I have to take the fight to them. I can't let them dictate how it will happen. I know this valley, so I have the advantage. I want you to stay here and stay inside. Do not go outside for any reason. There is enough wood and food here to last you until I get back. They must not know you are here; do you understand?"

"But I thought I could," Molly started.

"Well, you thought wrong. Keep your weapons handy just in case, but I don't intend they ever get this far. In the unlikely event something should happen to me, you can get out of here on your own. You know the way, and I know you can make it. You're strong and smart. Just make sure you aren't being followed."

Molly was not happy with the decision Dal had apparently made all by himself, but knew it was futile to argue. She asked, "how are you going to handle this?"

"I'm going to go back down the valley. I'll stick to the Northernmost side next to the rocks and cliffs so it will be more difficult to be spotted. When I get to where we left last night, I'll see what they are up to. Maybe I can discourage them before it comes to a full-fledged fight. Could you please pack me some food in that small pack? I want to travel as light as possible, but still have supplies just in case I can't make it back tonight."

Molly turned and did as Dal had asked without a word. Dal could see she was disappointed she wouldn't be going along, but he didn't want to risk her being hurt or worse. She filled the pack with various supplies and handed it to him.

"Dal, I want you to promise me something," Molly stated.

"What?" Dal asked as his eyes met hers.

"Promise me you'll come back." Her eyes held his for several seconds, and he could see tears welling up and then overflowing down her cheeks. The only thing in the entire world that made him weak in the knees was to see a woman cry. He reached out and drew her to himself and just held her as he felt her body racked with sobs.

"I promise I'll come back, Molly," he whispered into her hair. "No matter what, I'll come back."

They stood locked in each other's embrace, lost in the moment, knowing this was a turning point in their relationship. Neither one wanted to release the other, but it was Dal who finally made the move. "I have to get going. I have to make the most of the light there is left. Remember what I said about not going outside. When I get back, I'll make the sound of a mourning dove, twice. When you hear that, you'll know I'm here, and you can unbar the door. Don't worry about me, I'll be fine."

He took the pack and strapped it on his back, picked up his gun and powder, checked his knife, and turned to face Molly. She stepped up to him and they kissed. Lightly at first, then with passion and urgency. When their lips parted, Dal was stunned. He had never before in his life felt like he did right now. It took all the will-power he could muster to back away and go out the door, leaving Molly standing there in the middle of the castle.

"Bar the door," he called after him, and he was gone.

Molly was far from surprised at what had just happened. She had known her feelings for him were of this nature. She had only been waiting for him to find out how he felt about her! She had known for some time now that he was the man she wanted to spend the rest of her life with. Now, it seemed he might know that too!

Dal made his way carefully along the base of the rocky cliff and followed it down toward the Eastern end of the valley. If he could make it down there undetected, he could see what they were up to, and then plan his strategy. He had to admit he was by no means just a little shaken up by what had just happened between him and Molly. Oh, he had known he had some feelings for her and there had been some sparks here and there along the way, but wow! Suddenly, it occurred to him that he was in love with Molly! A blizzard of thoughts hit his brain all at once, and though he was cautious of where he was going, he failed to see two tiny black specks on the snow about a mile off on his left hand. Those two tiny specks were Jake and Bill, and though they failed to see Dal, they were headed straight for the castle. Of course, they did not know the castle even existed for they had not seen it on their way into the valley. Only about a half mile more would put them within sight of the castle, if they indeed would even notice it.

Dal kept his course straight for the campsite of the night before, and because he had snowshoes, made good time, and was there within three hours. Cautiously he made his way to where he and Molly had spent part of the night and then made their escape in the snowstorm in the middle of the night. When he got there, he found Frank's body covered with snow. He uncovered it just enough to see he had been shot and stripped of any valuables. Dal covered him back up with snow and then proceeded to try and figure out what had happened here. He slowly made a wide circle and found where the five men had split up and converged on the campsite from all different directions. This guy must have been shot by one of his own men. But why? That question would possibly never be answered. Next, he saw where they had gathered around and probably discussed their plan, and then taken different directions. Two going South, and two going West. Why hadn't he seen those who went West? Could they have possibly gotten by him without him seeing them? He mulled this over in his brain for a few minutes and troubling though the thought was, he didn't think that was possible. Surely, he would have seen them along the way. The valley was not that wide. He certainly would have seen them. He was a little worried about Molly, but as long as she stayed put inside the castle, there was little chance she would be discovered unless they actually walked right up to the door.

He decided he should scout farther South and see what these two guys were up to, since he was this close, and then he would check on the other two. He was never one to dilly dally around after his mind was made up, so he was off without another thought. He would track these two and if need be, dispatch them before heading back up the valley. Nobody intruded into his valley with thoughts of doing him harm without paying the price! The sun was now at his back as he headed farther down the valley.

The tracking was easy, and he saw five horses digging in the snow for grass just a short distance from where the dead man lay. They scarcely paid him any attention as he made his way past them. He noticed their poor condition and decided right then what type of men he would be dealing with. Most any who had spent any time in the mountains knew that if you had a horse, and depended on that horse to get you around, you always made sure they were taken care of. These horses were skin and bones, and Dal knew those who owned them were selfish, uncaring men, who would show no mercy to anyone they came in contact with. He had seen their type before and knew what lay before him. So be it. They never should have wondered into his valley They would pay dearly for their intentions.

He made good time as he closed the distance on his new enemies. Very few men could match the pace he now set as he determined to deal with whatever lay ahead of him, however he was totally alert to his surroundings, his senses on edge for any movement or sound that was foreign. Soon, he came to an area of dense brush covered ground that once was an old beaver pond. He had trapped here two winters in a row, but the beavers had moved upstream, as was their nature, after they had run out of trees for their food and construction of dams. It seemed strange that just a few short years ago, this land had been voided of any trees due to the extensive work of the beavers in the area, and now it was so thick with head-high bushes it was hard to walk through. The tracks he had been following led right into the thickest of bushes. To follow them into that could mean he would be walking into a trap. He wouldn't be able to see them until he stepped on them. Dal decided he would skirt around the bushes as best he could. This way he could continue to wear his snowshoes, and he could also see if the tracks continued beyond this extremely large stand of alders. He slowed his pace and worked his way around to the right of the bushes, being careful not to make any undue noises. Little did he know he was being watched by two sets of eyes from inside the thicket.

John and Wayne had made their way inside the stand of alders and found the old beaver dam that used to have this whole area flooded. After the beavers had deserted this dam, the spring run-off had broken a hole in the dam and the water had drained out, leaving the area once again, dry. They had decided to stop and rest for a spell and have a bite to eat of the already cooked meat they carried in their packs. Scarcely had they finished with their meal when they were aware of movement outside the thicket. They had hunkered down behind an old beaver house and peered out through the stems of bushes. Vaguely they could see the shape of a very large man stalking the edge of the thicket. They stayed right where they were, hardly daring to even breathe.

Slowly the shape of the man disappeared from their view. They looked at one another and Wayne was the first to speak in a hushed tone. "What do ya think we should do?"

John answered him in a whisper, "we need to take him by surprise, and we need to make our shots count."

"O.K.," answered Wayne, "but now is the time to make our move. We can come out behind him and plug him before he even knows we're here."

"Let's go," agreed John.

Slowly they crept out from behind the beaver house and edged their way toward the place they had last seen the man. As they came to the edge of the thicket, Wayne stuck his head slowly out to see if he could catch sight of the one they were now stalking. Sure enough, not a hundred yards away, the man was fiddling with his snowshoes, trying to tighten the harness on one of them. Wayne motioned for John to follow him into the opening, at the same time whispering, "we need to shoot this here coon before he knows we are here. Otherwise, I'm thinking we're gonna have a fight on our hands. Let's get out into this opening and take a bead on him. When I give the signal, shoot."

They both made their way into the opening and stood up, shouldering their rifles, and taking aim on Dal, whose back was still to them. They had no problem shooting a man in the back. It was easier that way.

It's hard to say what told Dal that he was not alone, but he suddenly became aware that there were eyes on him. Instinctively, he stood to his feet and sidestepped as best he could with the snowshoes attached to his feet, at the same time turning and taking in the entire scene at a glance. This action bought him some time,

136

be it only a couple of seconds, because it took John and Wayne totally by surprise. And because it took them by surprise, they were not able to make a well-placed shot. Their rifles roared as one as Wayne shouted, "shoot." One load took Dal in the left shoulder, and the other just under the rib cage on his right side. Dal was knocked back by the impact and he lost hold on his own weapon, which fell beyond his reach as he fell to the ground. He knew he was hurt bad and that he had to retrieve his gun if he were to live. They would be coming up on him any second and would probably finish him off, but try as he might, he couldn't move. His left arm was useless, and the bullet in his right side made it impossible for him to reach for his rifle. He was utterly at their mercy. He could feel himself losing consciousness, and fought to stay awake, but to no avail. Slowly he drifted into blackness.

Wayne and John made their way cautiously to where Dal lay unconscious in the snow. When they reached him, they were taken aback.

"We know this guy," whispered John incredulously.

"We sure do," agreed Wayne. "I never thought we'd see him agin."

"Ya don't look so tough now big guy." shouted John as he poked at Dal with his rifle. They both recalled that day many years before when they had been tormenting that girl and this big lout had come to her rescue, blackening their eyes and cutting their lips with his ham sized hands.

"Yeah, why don't ya get up and fight now big shot?" yelled Wayne. He lashed out with a kick to the side with the bullet hole. Dal groaned even in his unconscious state which brought laughs from both John and Wayne.

"What was that girl's name, do ya remember?" asked John.

"Yeah, I remember. Her name was Molly. She sure was pretty. I wanted her bad and would've had her if this jerk hadn't shown up," answered Wayne.

"What do ya say we put a bullet through his skull, jest fer old time's sake? Said John.

"Well now thet sounds jest fine to me, 'ceptin' I'm thinking maybe we ought to leave 'im here for the wolves," sneered Wayne.

"Hey now that sounds mighty nice to me," agreed John. "Why don't we jest take his rifle and knife and get back to our rendezvous with Jake an' Bill? They'll be right happy to hear the good news."

"O.K.," said Wayne, "but you can carry 'em yourself. I'm a carryin' all I'm agoin' to."

"I ain't carryin' nothing'," retorted John. "I reckon he ain't in no shape to use either one of em. Jest toss 'em over yonder. He's as good as dead anyway."

Wayne collected Dal's rifle and his knife and tossed them into the edge of the alders, and taking one last kick at Dal, they headed for the rendezvous point with Jake and Bill.

Chapter Seventeen

D al remained unconscious for the better part of the afternoon. He gradually became aware of things around him, and he lay there listening, trying to determine if he was alone or if they were still there, waiting for him to come around so they could torture him or finish him off. He slowly opened his eyes and grimaced as he realized the wounds he had sustained. His left shoulder was on fire and his right side ached something fierce. He tried moving his left hand, and seeing that he could, he tried moving his entire arm. Painfully, he moved it inch by inch until he could reach across with his other hand and lift his arm onto his torso. He realized that he had to get out of this snow and, if possible, kindle a fire so he wouldn't freeze to death. He knew he would have to spend at least one night here and try to get himself patched up. He always carried supplies in his pack for just such emergencies, and he had to get that off his back so he could get to them. He summoned his remaining strength and sat up. The world spun before his eyes, and he thought he was going to slip into unconsciousness again. He closed his eyes and gritted his teeth waiting for the dizziness to pass. When it finally did, he was able to get his pack and retrieve the supplies he needed to patch up those bullet holes. He had never been shot before, but had seen others who had, and as he evaluated his wounds, he determined that they were not as bad as they felt. The bullet to the shoulder had passed straight through. All he had to do was make sure the bleeding was stopped, pack it with some dried moss, and bandage it tightly. He had some extra strips of leather he could make a sling with to help immobilize his arm until it had started to heal.

This done, he turned his attention to the hole in his right side. This bullet also had passed through and had missed hitting anything vital. Lucky, he thought, and immediately he knew it hadn't been luck. He had always believed there was a God, and now he was sure of it. He had definitely looked out for him today! If either bullet had been an inch one way or the other, he would have been dead right now. He wasn't sure why they hadn't finished him off when they had the chance, but he was surely grateful for another chance at life.

He cleaned the wound as best he could and packed it with some of the same moss he had used on his shoulder wound and put a bandage over the entrance and exit holes, wrapping another piece of rawhide around his middle and tying it tightly to hold the bandage in place. Now he had to get onto his feet and get into the protection of the thick alders where he could find some dry wood to make a fire with. Pain wracked his body as he came to his feet and he staggered, almost falling back to the ground. He braced his feet and stayed upright, and then, taking tiny steps, reached the edge of the thicket where he could hold onto the bushes to steady himself. He would have to take the snowshoes off because the bushes were too close together for him to walk with them on. Holding on with his good arm, he allowed his left arm to dangle in front of him and bent over to where his fingers could undo the snowshoes from his feet. It took him quite a few minutes to accomplish this, and when done, he was totally exhausted. He knew, however, that he couldn't stop now. His life depended on getting into the thicket and putting together a fire. This would require wood enough to last through the night. He was able to walk fairly easily through the bushes, holding on with his good arm, and he was absolutely amazed that as he entered the alder thicket, there on the ground, were his rifle and knife! He couldn't believe they hadn't taken them with them! Stooping over, he retrieved his knife first. This was the knife his father had given him before he had come to the mountains, and it meant a lot to him. Its gleaming blade and bone handle with the carved wildlife scenes on it were in as good a shape now as the day it had been given to him. He placed it in its sheath on his belt and then reached down and got his rifle. This rifle had been the one he had worked so hard and saved his money for back home. He had shot his first deer with it.

Now he had to tend to the business at hand and get a fire going. He began to search around for dry wood, and was rewarded with a pile of sticks that the beavers had placed on top of another one of their houses. It was high enough to be out of the snow. Dal busied himself with retrieving all the wood he could and arranging it for a fire. He had some dry moss left over and some shavings in his pack, that he always carried for just such situations. He placed these under the wood and struck his flint, sending a spark into the moss, igniting it almost instantaneously. The flame got brighter and continued to grow until he had a good-sized fire going. It warmed him, and some of the stiffness began to leave his body. He sat down on a fallen tree and leaned his back against the bushes. Gradually, he began to relax, and as the heat from the fire penetrated his tired, aching muscles, he felt himself slipping into much needed sleep. He was pretty confident that his fire would not be seen outside the thicket, and he was sure these attackers wouldn't be back since they had left him to die. He just needed rest and time for his body to start the healing process. Tomorrow he would plan his course of action. His head rolled forward onto his chest, and he was asleep, oblivious to anything around him.

The sun had sunk below the horizon, and it was almost dark when Jake and Bill, John and Wayne regrouped back at Frank's frozen corpse. Wayne could hardly wait to tell the other two what had happened.

"Hey Bill, you remember that coon thet stopped us from taking that Molly girl back in the settlements?" Wayne asked.

"Yeah, I remember," Bill answered, his weariness showing through.

"Well, this guy we've been after is the same one!" John said before Wayne could answer.

"Are ya sure ya know 'im" asked Jake?

"Yeah, we're sure. We jest shot 'im and got a real good look at 'im," said Wayne barely able to contain his excitement.

"Did ya kill 'im?" asked Jake.

"Well not right then, but he's as good as dead with two holes in 'im. We figured he'd make good wolf bait." laughed John.

"You boys'd better hope he don't survive. 'Cause if'n he does, he'll be after ya hides with a vengeance," replied Jake as he pointed a finger at each of them.

"Aw, he weren't so tough," snickered Wayne. "That lead softened him up pretty fast, and I've got more where thet one came from!"

"Hey, if'n he were down this end of the valley, whar in tarnation is his squaw?" asked John. "He must've left her somewhar stashed away out of sight."

"Yer right," replied Jake. "And all we have to do is find 'er. Come morning, we'll spread out across the valley an' make a sweep to the tother end, and we'll jest find this here little squaw."

"Thet sounds like a good plan," said Wayne with a sneer on his face.

They all agreed with Wayne and then without another word, they went to retrieve their horses that were only a short distance away, and then proceeded to dig a hole in the snow for a fire and a place they could hunker down out of the wind that had begun to blow from the Northeast. They knew it would be a cold night, and so firewood was gathered and placed in a pile within easy reach of where they would camp for the rest of the night. They still had a fair-sized piece of meat left in one of their saddlebags, so they spitted that and hung it over the fire to cook. Soon the aroma of venison was making their mouths water. The coffee pot was set in the edge of the fire to heat water for their coffee. John got the coffee grounds from his saddlebag and added them to the pot when the water was boiling.

"Thet's the last of our coffee," he informed the others.

"We'll have more by tommora night," chuckled Jake, as he took the cut of meat from the fire and divided it into four equal pieces. "When we find this coons camp, and his squaw, we'll not only have more supplies, but we'll also have somebody to fix it fer us!"

The others all laughed loudly at this and then began to wolf down the meat and wash it down with the coffee. When they finished, they all got their bedrolls from off the back of their saddles and arranged them around the fire where they could stretch out and, being below the level of the snow, remain relatively warm.

Soon they were relaxing in their beds, and slowly, one by one they drifted off to sleep, their snores echoing around the fire.

Up at the end of the valley, Molly was growing sleepy after a long day of busying herself with small jobs around the castle and trying not to worry about the man she had just recently realized that she was in love with. But try as she would, she couldn't help but wonder where he was, and if he was alright. Even though Dal was a seasoned mountain man, she knew he was not invincible, and would never be able to relax completely until he was back at her side once more.

Tomorrow, since she had completed all the tasks she had planned to do inside, she decided she would venture out and see what needed doing around the front of the castle. She would also rearange the meat storage room so it would be easier to see what was available at a glance.

She climbed into bed and covered herself with the newly resown furs and drifted off to sleep with thoughts of Dal in her head. Never had she known a man who stirred the feelings like he did.

Chapter Eighteen

At the opposite end of the valley, a lone figure sat leaning against the bushes at his back, his fire dying down to just coals. Dal slowly came awake and, for a moment, could not remember where he was. He was cold, and he shivered involuntarily, pain wracking his body, as he gradually recalled the events leading up to this time. His arm was stiff, and his side burned as he reached with his good arm and put some wood on the almost dead coals. The wood was bone dry, and it caught, flames slowly growing until it was a roaring fire once again. The heat penetrated Dal's body and he was able to relax and think about what course of action he needed to take in the morning. He knew he needed to get back to Molly as soon as possible, but he would need to proceed with caution, for he knew these men would now be searching for her. They would know she was at the Western end of the valley, and they would be looking intently for her. The one advantage he had, was that they would presume him dead or unable to put up a fight.

This was not the worst shape he had ever been in, and he knew he could work through the pain. All he needed was as much sleep as he could get tonight, and a good meal in the morning. It would definitely be a challenge to get moving, but he could do it. He was motivated by his newfound love for the woman who waited for him now. He would not be satisfied until she was safe at his side once more. He knew there was no danger threatening him tonight, so he could relax totally. With these thoughts in mind, he drifted off to sleep, resting once again against the alders at this back.

The first rays of the morning sun reached high into the sky illuminating the clouds with brilliant red and orange hues. Dal wakened from his deep sleep, with sore aching muscles and pain in both areas where he had sustained the gunshot wounds. Looking at the sky, Dal knew this day would bring snow to the valley. Hopefully this would work to his advantage, hiding his tracks from those who had become his enemies. He slowly worked his arms, extending them out in front of him, opening and closing his hands, then bending his elbows and bringing his arms close to his chest. Several minutes of this, loosened his arms up so he had almost the entire use of his left arm again. His side, though still very sore and tender to the touch, would not really prevent him from doing what needed to be done, unless he had to resort to hand to hand combat.

This, he knew, could prove to be disastrous if he got hit or kicked there, but he would have to take his chances.

He reached down, purposefully with his wounded arm, and retrieved firewood and placed it on the bed of coals that still glowed brightly at his feet, and then he rummaged in his backpack for something to eat that would help restore some of the strength he would so badly need before this day ended. He wasn't sure what remained for food, but was rewarded by finding some biscuits Molly had packed for him, and a good amount of pemmican. This was packed with nutrients and protein that would help him in the fight that was sure to take place. The heat once again warmed him and helped relax his body, as he ate his breakfast. Every move he would make this day, would be slow and calculated, for he dare not rush into any situation that would further endanger him or Molly. Though he knew Molly could be in danger right now, he refused to give in to the urge to rush to her defense. He had complete confidence that she was capable of taking care of herself in any situation, and he was confident in his own abilities in facing enormous odds and coming out on top. He knew he could rescue Molly if it came to that. Hopefully, he would get there before she needed rescuing.

He finished his morning meal and washed it down with snow. No time for coffee this morning! He picked up his rifle and checked it to make sure it was ready to fire when the time came, and he had no doubt that time would come! His knife, he made sure was securely in its sheath on his belt. From his pack, he took the pistol that was rolled in a piece of tanned leather, checked the load in it, and placed it in his belt as well. Standing, he kicked snow on the fire and retrieved his snowshoes he had left standing against the alders the previous night. He made his way out of the thicket, standing in the edge long enough to peer one way and then the other to be sure he was alone. Satisfied he was, he emerged into the open, strapped on his snowshoes, and stood for a moment getting his bearings. Then, with long, slow strides he started up the valley toward Molly, and who knew what else?

Farther West, another camp was coming to life. Jake, Bill, John, and Wayne stirred, and one by one rolled out of their robes. Each one anticipated what this day would bring, and they were excited to think they would have a squaw in their camp come nightfall. Somewhere she was holed up, and they would find her. Of this, they were certain. All they had to do was find the tracks left by the man and follow them right to where she was. While each one was thinking of what good luck they had had, in the shooting of the giant, and his probable death during the night, Jake was the first to break the silence. "All we have to do, is find his tracks, and follow them right to his camp. We know that since me an' Bill stayed on the North side and didn't see him, he must've come down on the South side. So, what we'll do, is fan out over on the South side 'til we find his snowshoe tracks."

"What're we gonna eat fer breakfast? Our coffee is gone, and we et the last of our meat last night fer supper," complained Bill.

"Well," answered Wayne, "I reckon we'll just have ta wait'n eat with our squaw. We'll see what kind of a cook she is." They all laughed raucously at this and busied themselves with rolling up their bedrolls. The horses had stayed close to camp last night, so it was an easy task to catch them and saddle up. The few days off along with the grass they had been fortunate enough to find had allowed some of their strength to return, and they were eager to get back on the trail.

Over confidence, many times has led to the demise of whole armies down through history. A feeling of having everything under control, with no obstacles to face. Such was the case with these four men as they headed West up the valley. Their biggest threat had been removed, or so they thought, and now they were free to pursue, what they felt, was their reward for the whole ordeal they had suffered this winter. All they had been through, was now going to pay off. It was all going to be worth it.

As they started out, they stayed in single file, for it was easier on the horses to let one break the trail through the deep snow, and the others follow. They would swap point positions as they proceeded up the valley, so one horse didn't have to do all the work. Education in the mountains, was a hands on, make or break class. Only the best passed the course. This group of men had survived more than half of this winter. They had faced obstacles that had toughened and hardened them both physically, and mentally. It could be argued, however, that some of this had been by accident rather than skill.

They had ridden for just under an hour, each one having taken the lead once, when Jake ordered a halt. "We'll rest the horses here fer a spell, and then head South to find his tracks. They won't be hard to spot, 'cause he was a wearin' snowshoes. He must've stayed close to the rocks so's we couldn't spot 'im."

"How far you figure it is afore we find this here squaw, Jake?" asked Wayne.

Jake, who had been standing at the head of the group looking up the valley, turned to face the others. "Well, I reckon we're less'en halfway up the length of this here valley. So, I'm a thinking we might make it around noon," Jake replied with confidence in his voice.

"Thet sounds good to me. I'm 'bout starving, and I sure could use a cup of hot coffee," Bill said from the back of the group.

"I say we close in fast and git this over with," said John as he smacked his fist into the palm of his other hand. This brought grunts of approval from Wayne and Bill.

Jake shook his head and spoke sharply, "we have to proceed with caution. I've seen squaws and what they kin do with a bow and arrows. They kin be about as hard to handle as a sow grizzly with cubs! If'n we jest charge right in, one or more of us jest might lose our hair! We're gonna take our time an' scout things out a'fore we just walk right in. When we git closer to the end of the valley, John an' Bill, I want you two to split off n me an' Wayne, and take the North side. We should meet at the middle of the valley right at the end where that there cliff rises up. Remember the one we seen when we came in?"

Both John and Bill acknowledged with a grunt and looked at each other with uninterested stares. They both wanted to just get this whole thing done with, taking for granted they would have much better living arrangements after they found this camp.

"Let's get goin' then, and remember, keep a sharp eye out. We don't know where she may be camped. It shouldn't be too hard to find, but with all these boulders, it could be hidden pretty good," warned Jake as he turned, mounted his horse, and started up the valley once more. The others did likewise without another word, following in single file.

A little farther on, Jake pulled his horse up and turning in his saddle, said, "this is whar' we'll split up. John and Bill, you boys go ahead an' head fer the North side of the valley. Me an' Wayne'll give ya' 'bout an hour's head start afore we move on. Thet should make it so's we meet in the middle of the valley under thet cliff. If'n we aint thar when you git thar, give us a few minutes and then come and find us. We'll do the same with you. If'n you find her camp, wait fer us to git thar. We want in on the excitement!" he winked.

John and Bill jerked on their horse's reins and spurred them in the direction of the Northern wall of the valley. The horses hesitated, not wanting to venture into the deep snow, but soon were plowing through snow almost up to their bellies.

Clouds had begun to roll in, and soon the sun had disappeared. A cold damp wind had begun to blow, and soon, snowflakes were dancing on the wind, increasing in intensity, until visibility was cut to only a few feet in front of them. Jake cursed their bad luck and hoped this was only a passing snow squall. Somehow, though, he knew it wasn't. This was settling in for another bad storm with significant accumulations. This would indeed hamper their search for this squaw and her

155

camp. He silently wondered to himself what the other two would do. Would they continue to move, or would they hole up somewhere? He guessed it didn't matter, since he had instructed them to come and find them if they weren't at the designated meeting spot. If they were foolish enough to keep moving, they would eventually find he and Wayne. All they had to do was stay along the rock wall. They couldn't get lost, even in this type of storm.

Right now, he and Wayne needed to find some shelter. Maybe along this wall, they would find some boulders that would at least keep the wind off them. Jake directed his horse toward the cliff that was barely visible in the distance through the swirling, blowing, snow. As they neared the cliff, he turned in his saddle and yelled to Wayne over the howl of the wind, "look for some boulders we can use fer shelter. We'll hole up an' wait this here storm out afore we go on."

"Sounds good to me," Wayne shouted back. "Looks like a good place right ahead of us." He pointed to some huge boulders that had broken loose from the face of the cliff sometime in the past and had come to rest in a sort of shelter, just a few feet apart. They appeared to be tall enough to provide shelter from the howling wind. Jake looked to where Wayne had pointed, and, seeing them, headed his horse in that direction. When they got to the huge rocks, they dismounted, and led the horses to the area between the wall and the boulders where they could be sheltered as well. Then the men went into the area inside the boulders and, using their feet, kicked snow up as high as they could in the gaps between the rocks, making it even more protected. In so doing, they also made a hole in the snow where they could hunker down, and with the furs used for bedrolls, they could remain somewhat warm and comfortable.

They had not heeded the signs Nature had shown them this morning. The red sunrise was a sure indication that snow was inevitable, but they had ignored that sign. Now here they were, stuck in a blizzard-like storm, with no wood for a fire, and no food to sustain them and give them energy. Once again, Jake cursed to himself for the bad luck.

Bill and John had reached the far wall of the valley after about an hour of travel. The snow was falling so thick they knew they had to find shelter soon. As they proceeded along the bottom of the towering wall of rock, they found a place similar to what Jake and Wayne had found. Soon they were under their furs, huddled together for warmth, the snow piling up on top of them. Before long, they were mounds of snow amongst the boulders, their horses facing away from the wind beside them.

In their minds, they each hoped this storm would not last very long, for if it continued like it was now, they would never be able to walk in it. Not even the horses could navigate through much more snow. They would be stranded here in this valley without any food or shelter. They would probably die here! Panic welled up in each of their hearts, and they wondered what they would do. What could they do?

Chapter Nineteen

Dal had made it back to where his trapline started before it had begun to snow very heavy. He had, unlike those who were caught in the snowstorm with no supplies, heeded the signs Nature had shown him this morning, and gotten some wood for a fire, and on inspection of some of his traps, found a rabbit in one of them. This he had promptly skinned and prepared the meat to roast over a fire when needed. He knew the storm was going to get bad, so he decided he would check the rest of his traps to make sure no animals stayed in them longer than necessary. He had already missed a couple days, and he felt badly because he never allowed his traps to go unchecked for more than a day. Circumstances had been out of his control however, but now he needed to check them.

He made his way from trap to trap finding most of them with a captive in each one. Foxes mostly made up the majority, but their pelts were prime, and Dal was glad he had taken the time to check them now rather than waiting for a later time. These pelts would help to fill out the bundles he already had, which would assure him of supplies for the next winter season. The time he spent here also allowed his wounds to heal more, and the exercise helped to loosen his tight, sore muscles. This would work in his favor when he encountered those men again. He had no doubts that he would indeed meet up with them again. This time it would turn out differently. He would not be the victim!

Dal had located a spot that would afford him the best possible shelter from the fast-approaching storm, and he now busied himself with starting a fire, and putting the rabbit carcass on a stick over the flames to cook. He got his coffee pot from his pack and, after adding snow to it, placed it in the edge of the fire to melt for water for his coffee. He stood his snowshoes up in the snow on the side of the fire the wind was coming from and took a fur from his pack that was an extra that he always carried for just such emergencies, and placed it over the snowshoes and tied it in place with rawhide thongs. This made a shelter from the wind that would help protect the fire and him during the long night ahead. He unrolled his bedroll and draped it over his shoulders to help warm him as he waited for the meat to cook. The smell of the roasting rabbit made his mouth water, as the water in his coffer pot began to boil. He added coffee to the water and sat back, in relative comfort, and thought about what he might be facing.

160

He knew there were four men. That in itself did not bother him. He had faced bigger odds before and pulled through. These particular men did not strike him as being too smart. He had seen their camp from the previous night. There had been no evidence of any food being cooked. There had been a very little fire, which meant they had not collected very much wood. Who in their right minds lived out here without the proper preparation for each and every day and night? Care had to be taken to make sure every need was addressed. To do otherwise was inviting disaster.

Even though they had shot him, he knew that had been because of his own carelessness. That would not happen again. If they shot him this time, it would be because they outsmarted him, and he doubted their ability to do that. He was not being arrogant or overly proud in his assuming these things. He merely was confident in his skills as a seasoned mountain man. He had survived these years in the mountains, not by luck, but by pure skill. Indians had not been able to acquire his scalp, though they had tried many times, so he knew these four were no match for him.

The rabbit was fully cooked, and the coffee was ready, so he set about eating his meal, happy to be beside a roaring fire. He wished Molly could be here with him. He missed her. Every time he thought about her, he got a strange feeling down in the pit of his stomach. He hated to admit it, but he knew he was in love with her. She had found a place in his heart, and he knew she was the one. Strange, how he had come to the mountains, never expecting to even see a white woman, let alone fall in love with her! God sure works in mysterious ways! Even these mountains couldn't keep them apart!

Having finished his meal, he checked his weapons, making sure the firearms were primed, and ready to fire. His knife was where it always was, on his belt in its own leather sheath, its blade honed to a keen edge. He had spent many a night beside a fire, whetting this blade until it was razor sharp. He took pride in this knife, because it was the one his father had given him a few years ago when Dal had told him he was heading to the mountains. He had fond memories of his family and vowed he would make it his way to get back there and see them again this summer. How long had it been since he had last seen them? He had to stop and think, but he thought it was going on about five years. He wondered if his sisters were married, and if so, how many kids would they have by now? That would make him an uncle! How were his mother and father doing? Yes, he would go see them all this summer!

The crackling fire and dancing flames never ceased to mesmerize Dal, and with a good hot meal under his belt, he settled into his bedroll, and was soon fast asleep, knowing that tomorrow would be the day of reckoning for these four men. They had invaded his valley; they had brought the fight to him; now they would have to pay the consequences.

It was not a normal thing that men should be out and about during the long winter months here in the mountains. Anyone, who had any mountain savvy, knew you had to stay pretty much in one camp during this time to avoid being caught in the open without any food or wood for a fire. Snow can get as deep as six or eight feet, and to be caught in that was sure death.

Dal had spent much time during the summer and fall months, collecting firewood enough to last through the winter. He had also spent much time during the latter part of the fall months, shooting game and preparing the meat for his cache'. There were a variety of different meats, including deer, elk, buffalo, and beaver tails. He had smoked some of this meat, and salted the rest, but knew that none of it would spoil because it was frozen, and in a safe spot inside the castle. It was in its own little room that did not get any heat from the main part of the room, and so remained frozen and within easy reach of anyone inside the castle. Because of this, and the water supply that ran through the middle of it, anyone could remain holed up inside the castle for months on end if needed. It was easily defended because of the commanding view of the valley which lay in front of it, and it was very difficult to see from anywhere in the valley, until one was almost on top of it. All anyone had to do was stay inside, keep the door and window shut, and chances were, no one would ever suspect you were there.

Molly sat beside the fire in the castle, warm and satisfied from the meal of deer meat she had just had. Her thoughts were about Dal, and she wondered where he was, and if he was alright. This was the third night since he had left to find the intruders, and she couldn't help but worry. She knew he could take care of himself, but being outnumbered always bore some risks that were not able to be controlled. Getting up from her seat, she busied herself by washing her tin cup and plate. She kept a pot of water on the fire, so she always had hot water for such things. Adding another stick of wood to the fire, she thought about all the work Dal had done here this past fall to get everything ready for the long winter, and he hadn't even known she would be here with him. He had done all this in preparation for himself, what would he do, she wondered, to provide for her?

She recalled their good-byes when Dal had left, and the kiss they had shared, and her face grew hot as she blushed involuntarily. This was the man for her! She had come all this distance, and had suffered so much at the hands of the Indians, just to meet this wonderful man! God surely worked in mysterious ways!

Molly stepped to the door and opened it just a crack, peering into the darkness. The snow was still falling, and it was piled high against the outside of the door. She couldn't see more than a few feet, so she closed the door and decided it was time for bed. She doused the light and climbed under the robes, falling asleep almost immediately, only to dream about the man who had stolen her heart.

As morning approached, the snow tapered off to just a flurry, the wind died down, and as the sun poked its nose over the edge of the rock walls that bordered the valley, the clouds began to dissipate. Dal stirred in his robes and opened his eyes to a new day. He placed more wood on his fire and the hot coals soon turned to flames as the dry wood caught almost immediately. He would have a good breakfast, for he didn't know if he would eat again today. That depended on how events unfurled. He hoped, in the back of his mind, he could deal with these men quickly, and get back to his normal life here in his valley. "Normal," he thought, as he chuckled to himself. Life would be anything but normal with Molly around! But hey, normal can be kind of boring!

He had kept his weapons under his robes close to him during the night, so he knew they were not wet or needing to be checked again. But out of habit and instinct, he checked them anyway. Satisfied they were ready for whatever lay ahead, he ate his breakfast, which consisted of more meat, some pemmican, and coffee to wash it all down with. His belly being full, he placed what was left over inside his pack, along with the rest of his supplies, rolled up his robes, strapped on his snowshoes, and started his trek up the valley through the new snow. At least two or maybe three feet had fallen during the night. It was difficult to tell, because the wind had blown it into drifts several feet deep all along the valley floor. He stayed toward the Southern wall of the valley, and the drifts weren't quite as deep here. He was thankful for his snowshoes, and wondered how anyone would walk through snow this deep without a pair. Even a horse would have a difficult time breaking trail in this.

As he slowly made his way along the bottom of the rock wall, his senses were at full alert. His eyes were constantly moving so as to detect even the slightest movement, and his ears strained to hear any sound foreign to the area. Even his nose was trying to pick up some smell, be it smoke, horse, or man.

Jake slowly came awake to darkness, and thought for a moment, it was still night. He tried to move, but felt like something heavy was holding him down. Slowly it dawned on him that he was under his robe being weighed down by the snow that had fallen during the night. He wiggled this way and that, gradually shaking the snow from off his robe, until he was able to stand. He was greeted by bright morning sun that, for a moment, blinded him. He turned to face away from the sun, and gradually his eyes adjusted to the light till he was able to see what lay before him. He couldn't believe his eyes when he saw how much snow had accumulated. What lousy luck! Now they would have to plow their horses through even more snow. They still didn't have any supplies, so there would be no breakfast this morning. Not even a cup of coffee! He shivered as the cold, crisp, air hit him. The snow had insulated them during the night from the frigid temperatures. And now, with the clouds moving out, the temperature was dropping fast. He knew something had to be done fast. They had to find shelter, firewood, and food.

He looked around for a mound of snow, indicating where Wayne was huddled under the snow. Locating what must be him, he gave the mound a kick. Wayne came to with a start, and was on his feet in an instant, not knowing what had happened. His hand dropped to the knife on his belt aa he whirled to face whoever, or whatever was there. Jake saw him grab his knife and side-stepped out of Wayne's reach, at the same time yelling, "hold on thar Wayne, it's Jake!"

Wayne blinked as the sun blinded him as it had Jake, and he stood there with the knife out in front of him, poised for whatever was there. When he heard Jake speak, he turned to face him, and recognition slowly registered on his face. He slowly lowered the knife, placing it back in the sheath. "Sorry, Jake. I didn't know where I was, or who you was, thar fer a minute. It felt like I was bein' held down by something. What was thet?"

Jake, gesturing with his hand, said, "take a look around and you'll see what was weighing ya down."

Wayne swiveled his head and looked around them, his eyes widening at the sight of all the snow. "This is gonna slow us down considerable, Jake," he stated.

"Yeah, I was jist thinking the same thing. We need to find some shelter and food fast. The temperature is droppin' fast and we ain't had no food now since yesterday morning. We jest caint survive like this fer very long."

They found the horses where they had left them, saddles still on them, their heads hanging low. The men took hold of the reins and led the horses out into the open away from the boulders that had given them at least partial shelter during the night. The sun's rays extended the entire length of the valley, and the brightness on the new fallen snow made them squint. They mounted their horses, knowing they would not be able to walk through it on foot, and also knowing the horses would have a time of it as well. Progress would be slow, but they had to meet Bill and John up at the head of the valley.

Across the valley on the North side, the scene was almost exactly the same as on this side. One by one, first John, and then Bill came awake, not being able to move at first because of the snow on top of them. John realized almost immediately what had happened, but Bill almost lost it when he couldn't move. He began to yell and scream incoherently, until John kicked the snow off him so he could stand up. His eyes were wild, and he was gasping for breath as he came out of his robes, but as soon as he saw John, he quieted down.

"You O.K. thar Bill?" questioned John, as he tried to suppress a laugh.

Bill saw John laugh and said, "it ain't funny, John. That was scary, not being able to move and all."

"Sorry, Bill. You should've seen yer face, though. You looked like you'd seen a ghost!" chuckled John. Looking around at the snow, he said to Bill, "we have to get movin' so's we kin meet up with Jake an' Wayne. I think the horses are gonna have a hard time gittin' through this snow."

"I sure wish we had some grub and coffee," whined Bill. "I'm hungry."

John, while leading his horse into the open, turned and spoke to Bill, "yeah, I'm hungry too, Bill. We gotta git us some food before today is gone, or we won't be needin' any tomorra."

Bill shuddered at the thought and led his horse after John. Soon, they were making their way toward the end of the valley, the horses picking their way between drifts. Sometimes there was no way between them however, and they had to struggle right through the middle of one, snow up to the horse's bellies, threatening to hold them fast in its grip. Sometimes the men had to hold their feet up to keep them out of the snow. The horses tired quickly, and the men had to rest them frequently, so their progress was very slow to say the least. Progress, however, was made, and they neared the end of the valley at just about dinner time. The sun was straight overhead but did little to lessen the cold. It permeated the very being of man and beast.

Chapter Twenty

Molly woke as the sunlight flooded the valley and got out of bed to a chill that she had not felt before here in the castle. She knew it must have been extremely cold last night, because there was still some heat coming from the bed of coals in the center of the room. She pulled a deerskin dress on over her head and was glad for the warmth it provided her. She lighted the lamp in the corner to afford her more light here inside the castle. When having to keep the window shade closed, it didn't allow much light from outside to shine in, even though the sun was shining brightly. She would have much preferred the sunlight to that of the lamp, but she did not dare to open the shade, which fit on the outside of the window, and was attached from within, for fear it might possibly give her position away to anyone looking closely. When the shade was in place, it blended nicely with the rock face that made up the front wall of the castle. It never failed to amaze her how, when you got more than several feet away from the door and window, you could barely discern the wood from the rock. Someone had taken great precautions to make this place as inconspicuous as possible, and she was indeed grateful for that. She felt safer here than she had ever felt in her entire life, and she enjoyed that feeling. Some of that feeling of security, she knew, was due to Dal.

She wondered what he was doing right now. Had he found those men he had gone in search of, and if so, why wasn't he home yet? She felt certain that he must have found them at the other end of the valley. Probably he was on his way home right now. He would have spent last night holed up waiting for the storm to pass. He probably would be here at any time with an appetite as big as a grizzly just out of his den after a long winter nap! As she thought about that, she realized she would need to put a fair sized roast over the fire to slowly cook in preparation for his arrival. She went to the cache' of meat and found the perfect cut of meat, a choice cut of elk that Dal had smoked last fall. She brought it out and skewered it over the fire where it could cook over the next few hours.

Molly had always been one to keep her house, teepee, castle, whatever it was, clean, so she straightened up the chairs, pulled the robes over the top of the bed, and took care of the dishes she had left near the fire to dry after washing them last night. With that done, she sat on the edge of the bed and wondered what she would do next. She was getting bored just staying inside, and she wished she could take her snowshoes and explore parts of the valley she had not seen before. Dismissing this as far too dangerous, she decided that she could, however, move the snow from in front of the door, so when Dal came home, he wouldn't track any more in than necessary. She would not venture outside, only far enough as to be able to shovel snow away from the door that the wind had drifted against it last night.

Taking her fur coat from its peg on the wall, Molly retrieved the shovel Dal had made from the corner, and stepped to the door. She pushed the latch up and slowly opened the door, at first just a crack, but then enough so she could begin moving the snow. She would only move it to one side and arrange to look like the other snow that had fallen from the face of the wall. This didn't take her more than ten minutes, and then she was back inside, with the door closed, safe and secure once more. "Sure," she thought to herself, "here I am all comfy and Dal is out there somewhere in this cold." The more she thought about it, the more restless she became, until she knew she could not spend one more minute here without knowing whether or not Dal was O.K.

She put on the best furs she had to keep her warm, her fur-lined boots, hat, and mittens, all of which she had made herself while living with the Indians. Before gathering up her bow and arrows, she removed the roast from over the fire, and laid it on the table. Adding more wood to the fire, taking up her weapons, and snatching up her snowshoes, she went out the door without another thought about it.

Once outside, she stood for a minute letting her eyes get accustomed to the bright light, then squat down and strapped her snowshoes to her feet. She knew she needed to form a plan for her course of action, so she stood mulling it over in her mind what she should do, all the while looking down the valley, hoping to see that familiar giant figure coming her way.

Right now, her thoughts were more like an Indian than a white woman, for she had learned much while living with them. Things that could save her life in situations like she now faced. Her first thought was to find Dal, and to do this, she must venture East down the valley. She would stay close to the wall of the valley on the South side, so as not to be silhouetted against the snow out in the open, and she would need to keep a sharp lookout in every direction.

She had no idea from which direction the threat would come, but being ready for anything was her best defense right now. The bow and arrows were no match for rifles or pistols, but in close range, she was as good as any Indian buck! As a matter of fact, she had shown many of them up while she was a captive, and they resented it immensely. This had prompted much

174

verbal abuse, as well as physical abuse at the hands of the other squaws.

Only briefly thinking about this, caused her to shudder, and she immediately dismissed these thoughts from her mind and focused on the problem at hand. Slowly, but purposefully, she made her way through the deep snow, thankful she had the snowshoes to keep her on top. She only sunk in about a foot with each step, which was a whole lot better than three or four! She passed the spot where Dal had climbed the rocks and looked down the valley. It seemed like an eternity had passed since that day. She wished it hadn't snowed, so she could follow his tracks and located his whereabouts more easily, but she knew that would have made it easier for the enemy to find her and Dal.

She finally came to a spot where the rock wall curved away from the open area of the valley, and she couldn't see what was around the corner. As she remembered, there were several large boulders that had fallen from the rock wall in such a way as to make a shelter like formation. It would have made a good spot to weather the storm last night, and maybe Dal was here. Also, maybe someone else was here too!

She took the bow from around her neck and shoulder, and pulling an arrow from the quiver that hung on her back, nocked it on the bowstring, as she continued to make her way forward to where she could see around the corner.

There was about ten yards between her and the corner to where she could see what was on the other side. She had covered about half that distance when she thought she heard a horse blow behind her. She glanced around and to her horror, saw two men, mounted on horses following her tracks! They were still quite a distance away, and she wasn't sure if they had seen her yet or not. Slowly, so as not to draw any undue attention to herself, she made her way closer to the rock wall to make it more difficult for them to see her, and headed for those boulders where she could take a stand against these two intruders.

Once around the corner, she broke into a trot, careful not to catch a shoe and fall. She saw the boulders and headed for the closest one, unaware that other eyes were watching her from a considerable distance!

Chapter Twenty-One

B ill and John had gotten a pretty early start that morning, but because of the deep snow, the horses had not made very good time, struggling through drifts sometimes that threatened to bog them down. Consequently, they had to rest the horses many times. Due to their own lack of planning, two mealtimes had come and passed without any food. That, coupled with the slow pace, had their tempers on edge. They had long ago ceased talking, since they only bickered back and forth anyway.

Had they continued to the far end of the valley, they would have discovered Molly's tracks leading out of the castle, but instead, they had cut across the valley before reaching the end. Therefore, they had not seen the origin of the tracks they now followed.

It had been a satisfying discovery for Bill when he had seen the snowshoe tracks first. He had taken the lead position to give John's horse a breather from having to break trail, and as his horse had broken through yet another drift, there they were right in front of him. He, at first couldn't believe his eyes. He pulled his horse up and sat there rubbing first one eye and then the other, until John had caught up with him.

"Looky what I found, John," Bill said with an air of pride. He twisted in his saddle and watched as John came alongside him. "This must be that squaw. See, those tracks ain't sinkin' down very far in that snow. It must be her."

John sat his horse and looked down at the snow-shoe tracks. "I reckon you're right, Bill. She cain't weigh much mor'n a sack-a-grain. Jest whar you 'spose she be a goin' in all this here snow?"

"Cain't say as I'd be knowin' that, John, but all's we got to do is to folla these tracks, and we'll find her!" Bill answered him with satisfaction written all over his face.

"She's prob'ly lookin' fer her man. Too bad he's dead by now!" snickered John. "She'll be gittin' real lonely!"

"She won't be lonely too long," sneered Bill.

They spurred their horses onward as they followed the tracks that were so easy to follow. Soon they would overtake her, and she would be theirs. Now, they kept an eye on the terrain ahead of them. Had they been watching before they found the tracks, they would have seen Molly duck around the corner of the rock wall out of sight.

The eyes that had been watching from a distance, were those of Jake and Wayne. They had been making their way up the valley, expecting to see Bill and John, when, all of a sudden, they spotted a lone figure coming in their direction. They watched as it made its way closer, and then, as if startled by something, it had spun around and looked back. Then quickly it had gone closer to the wall and then headed for a group of boulders, taking refuge behind the first one. After disappearing behind it they no longer could see what was happening there. They did, however, see two horsemen approaching, and knew it was Bill and John.

Jake turned to Wayne and, in a hushed tone said, "they're following that squaw. I think she saw 'em and ducked in behind that boulder. If'n we can sneak up behind her, without her seein' us, maybe we can surprise her afore Bill and John git thar. I don't think they have even seen her yet."

Wayne squinted in the direction of the boulders and after a minute said, "That's a lot of open ground fer us to cover without her a seein' us. But I reckon even if she does, we've got her either way. She cain't git away now!"

"Well now, I reckon yer right thar' Wayne. Thar' really aint no reason to try an' sneak up on her. She aint no match fer the four of us!" Jake answered with confidence.

"C'mon, let's go git us a squaw!!" said Jake, as he started forward. His horse hesitated, not wanting to wade through another deep drift, but Jake drove his heels into the horse's side, and it plunged in, struggling to get through snow clear up to his belly. Wayne followed on his horse, and they slowly closed the distance between themselves and the group of boulders where Molly lay in wait for the two others. She had not seen Jake and Wayne approaching from behind her, so was unaware of the danger she was really in. Her eyes were focused on the wall where she knew they would appear at any moment following her tracks. She knew they would be in range of her bow when they rounded the corner. She would have to wait until they were in full view to give herself enough time to nock another arrow and dispatch the other rider. So intent was she on watching for the pair in front of her, she failed to notice the other two advancing on her position from the rear.

Soon enough, she saw the horse's heads appear. Then the rest of their bodies rounded the corner. The two men who sat them were watching in her direction, and past the boulders, they saw two more horsemen coming their way, and recognized them as Jake and Wayne. Bill raised his rifle over his head and let out a whoop in their direction.

Molly turned to see what he was signaling for and saw the other two approaching. What was she going to do now? She tried to think of what she *could* do. She was trapped! No matter what she did, they would get her! She decided the best thing she could do was give up peacefully, and maybe they would treat her better.

Her only hope now was for Dal to come to her rescue. And she hoped and prayed he would be fast in getting here! But, then again, she had really expected him to be back way before now. What if something had happened to him, and he wouldn't be coming back? What then? She would have to make her own escape. It would not be easy, but she had succeeded to get away from the Indians, and she doubted these men would be any harder to get away from.

Instinctively, she knew that she was in for a rough time. These men had probably not seen a white woman, or any woman for that matter, for a long, long time! They would be interested in only one thing, and she shuddered involuntarily as she thought about it and waited for the four men to close in on her.

Bill and John were the first to get to her, and she laid her bow and arrows at her feet. Molly watched them closely as they drew their horses to a stop and dismounted. She looked behind her, and the other two men were approaching also. If only she had seen these two sooner, she might have been able to defend herself from a different location.

Jake and Wayne made their way to the group of boulders where Molly and their partners now stood. Molly slowly raised her hands so they could see she held no weapons. John stepped forward and scooped up her bow and arrows. He stood, and slowly let his eyes wonder up and down her slim body. Something looked familiar about him, and as she tried to place where she had seen him before, he turned to Bill, and with a grin, replied, "hey Bill, looky what we found! Here is that squaw you been wantin' to meet!" As his eyes continued to rove up and down her frame, they finally came to rest on her face. Her blond her was not visible under her fur hat, but there was no hiding those blue eyes. He was shocked when suddenly he realized he was looking into the face of a white woman! "Wait a minute! This ain't no squaw!" he yelled, loud enough so Jake and Wayne heard him as they entered the group of boulders from the other direction.

"What ya' mean, she ain't no squaw?" asked Jake, walking to where she stood. He looked her up and down, and finally his eyes rested on hers as well. "Well, I'll be John!" exclaimed Jake. "You're right. She's a white woman!"

"What are you doin' out here, missy?" he asked Molly. "Yer supposed to be back in the settlements with all the other civilized women!"

Molly continued to look them in the face, but made no attempt to answer them. Her eyes never wavered as the men continued to stare at her.

Bill and John quickly joined the others to get a look at this woman. Their mouths were agape as they also, ogled her for several minutes, not saying a word.

Jake turned to Wayne and said, "Wayne, get a fire goin', we'll be campin' here fur the night. There should be some wood over along that treeline thar."

With the mention of that last name, Molly realized that three of these men were the same ones who had ambushed her and tried to have their way with her a few years earlier back in the settlements. Never would she forget their faces. She had been alone that day as well and had not noticed them coming along the road she was on until they were right there in front of her. And here she was again, in the same predicament, with the same ones, only now, they were grown men, just as she was a grown woman. She hoped they wouldn't recognize her, but she really hadn't changed in looks all that much. The only difference in her appearance was that now she had filled out where before she had been rather scrawny. They had poked and prodded her that day, ripping her dress in several places. There was no doubt what would have happened if that boy had not showed up when he did. It seemed he had just appeared from nowhere. Suddenly, he was pulling them off her, and slamming them to the ground one by one. It had seemed like he had no concern for his own wellbeing, as he took on all three, and scared them off.

After they had disappeared down the road, she had tried to thank him for what he had done, but he was painfully shy, and wouldn't even look at her. He had escorted her home, but would not go in. He simply turned and walked away, leaving her to watch after him, wondering who he was, or where he had come from. Not even to this day, did she know who he was. If only he were here now!

Jake once again broke the silence as he told Bill, "tie her up. And make sure she can't get loose. You other two, get the gear off the horses and make camp right here in these boulders. Tomorrow, we'll go find her camp, and make ourselves to home!"

Bill, having gotten some rawhide thongs from his saddlebags, approached Molly, and roughly tied her hands and then her feet. Even though he was the one who got spooked by a lot of things out here in the mountains, Bill was by far the most observant of them all. As he tied her up, he looked at her face and was reminded of a day long past when this same girl stood in front of him on a lonely stretch of road, just outside of a small town they had been passing on their way to help some family friends. Their fathers had arranged that they would help build a house and barn for these friends who had just arrived in the area.

They had met this girl, and one thing had led to another until the situation had gotten out of hand. Then, that other guy had shown up, the one they had just left for dead at the end of this valley, and given them a severe beating! Maybe this would end differently this time!

Molly tried not to look Bill in the eye as he tied her hands and then her feet securely, but she saw the look of recognition flash across his face, and she knew he remembered her.

As he straightened up from tying her feet, he looked directly in her eyes, and whispered, "your boyfriend ain't gonna be around this time to save ya'. He's layin' dead down at the end of this valley!" Turning, he went directly to his horse, and stripped the saddle from its back, and carried it into the circle of boulders. Each time he looked at her, he smiled cruelly.

Molly was stunned by his words. Could this really be? Could the boy who had saved her from these ruffians years before, be the same man who had rescued her from certain death in these mountains only a short few weeks ago? And what did he mean when he said that Dal was dead? Fear gripped Molly like never before. If he was indeed dead, all hope was lost for her. She had given herself up to them in anticipation of being rescued by Dal. Had she only known, she would have died defending herself rather than face what she knew was inevitable now.

She knew that if what this man had just told her was true, she was doomed to become a slave to these men, until they grew tired of her. Then she would be killed without regret, and no one would ever know her fate.

Bill had made his way to where the other three men were standing. They were talking about what they should do next. Jake was saying he thought they should use what daylight they had left to try and locate the camp that so far had eluded them.

John disagreed saying, "I think we should ought to stay right here tonight. We've got shelter from these here boulders, and firewood ain't too fer away neither. We been worse hungry before, and we can git a good early start in the morning."

Wayne and Bill both agreed with him, and so it was settled, even though Jake was not happy about it. They had all decided, after Frank had been killed, that they would take a vote on any decisions having to be made. Jake had agreed with that, and so now he must agree with this decision as well.

They set about making camp, each doing what needed to be done. Wayne and Bill went off in search of firewood for the night, John stripped the saddles from their horses as well as his own, bringing them into the circle of boulders, and arranging them around what would be the fire. Jake took the bridles from the horses and brought them into the circle as well. Normally, when the snow was not as deep, he would hobble the horses so they wouldn't stray too far from camp, but he knew they would not go away from where they were. They had enough of fighting the snow during the day. They would rest here, and dig to the bottom of the snow to get whatever they could to eat. Lately, they had not fared too well, and were getting dangerously thin. That was an issue they would have to address when they were snug in camp with their new woman. She would know where the best grasses grew during the summer months, and since they would have no need to use the horses any more this winter, they would let them loose to fatten up 'till Spring.

Having seen to the bridles, Jake went to where Molly was tied up, and squatted down in front of her. His eyes explored her face and then drifted down the length of her body. He decided she was a very beautiful woman. Her eyes were as blue as any sky he had ever seen. Reaching up, he slid the fur hat from her head, and was surprised when blond hair cascaded down her back and around her face. Since the time they had happened on the winter camp where this woman had met up with that giant of a man, Jake had thought she was an Indian squaw. All evidence had pointed to that. Never would he have thought a white woman would be in these mountains, not to mention one as stunningly beautiful as this! He had to admit, he was impressed that she could live here in this wilderness. Here she was, alone out here with just a bow and arrows. He would not feel confident with bow and arrows for his only weapons, and he had been in this environment for years.

He also noticed how her eyes never faltered under his scrutiny. Neither did she show any fear. She definitely had spirit. Deep down, he almost felt sorry for her, because he knew what lay ahead. It would not be easy for her, but he knew her spirit would be broken, just like a wild mustang whose spirit was broken, first to the lasso, and then to the saddle and bridle. Those that surrendered early, suffered far less than those who fought the rope. He had a feeling; this one would not give up easily.

Bill and Wayne busied themselves finding firewood for the night, and when they came back together, Bill said to Wayne, "did you notice anything about that woman?"

"Only thet she's pretty easy on the eyes." Wayne laughed.

"If'n you take a real good look at her, you'll see she's pretty familiar," Bill said.

"What ya' mean familiar?" asked Wayne.

"Remember thet gal on the road back in the settlements we chanced to meet, the one that guy we just killed rescued from us?" Bill asked, with a sneer on his face.

Even as Bill spoke, a look of understanding swept over Wayne's face. "How could we get so lucky?" he asked. "How did she ever end up here?"

"I don't know," answered Bill, "but we sure have some catchin' up to do! The rest of this here winter is gonna be jest pure heaven!"

"I sure am glad we took care a' that guy when we did. At least we don't have to worry about him interferin' with our fun agin," Wayne spoke with confidence.

Together they made their way back toward where they would be spending the night, their arms full of wood, and their spirit's light. As they entered the group of boulders, they deposited the wood near where Jake had scraped the snow away in preparation for the fire.

"We'll need 'bout twice that much to last us through the night," Jake announced. "You boys go git 'nother arm full."

Wayne ignored Jake and walked toward where Molly was seated in the snow, bound hand, and foot. Bill went to talk to John, and they were soon lost in conversation. Molly recognized Wayne as another one of the group of three boys who had accosted her that day, and tried not to show her concern as he approached her. To think that she had been spared the hurt and humiliation of that day years before, only to come face to face with the same group, now grown men, here in the wilderness, miles away from civilization. Her heart ached knowing that Dal was not able to help this time. He had given his life to try and save hers, and now she would face this trial alone. It was almost more than she could bare.

Even as these thoughts went through her mind, she vowed she would not give them the satisfaction of seeing her fear. She would remain strong just as she had while held captive by the Indians. There would come an opportunity when she could make her move, just as she had with the Indians. She only needed to wait patiently and watch for that opportunity. It might even come sooner than she anticipated.

Wayne knelt in front of her and just looked at her. Finally, he spoke to her in a hushed tone, "you ain't gonna be so lucky this time girly!" He edged closer until his face was only inches from hers. Their eyes locked until Molly spit full in his face. He jumped back, surprised as if he had been slapped. "You dirty squaw!" he screamed, as he raised his hand as if to hit her.

"Wayne!" yelled Jake. "Don't you even think about hitting her, or you'll have me to reckon with!" Wayne's hand remained raised, and it looked like he would hit her anyway. "Wayne!", Jake yelled again. This time there was an audible click as Jake cocked his pistol and pointed it at Wayne. His hand was slowly lowered, and he turned and stalked away from camp.

He would have his time with her, and she would regret what she had just done! He gave Jake a murderous look as he went to retrieve more wood. Bill tagged along behind, and they were soon out of sight of the camp.

Chapter Twenty-Two

Dal had been slowly making his way up the valley. He was taking his time to make sure no mistakes were made this time. He tried to learn from his mistakes, and he knew he had misjudged these men. He would not do so again. They would pay dearly for invading his valley and disturbing his life. He sincerely hoped they had not been successful in finding the castle, and Molly. He would, when he finally located them, observe their camp before making his move, to determine what he was facing. If, by some freak luck, they should have located the castle and Molly, it would be difficult to launch an attack. That place was virtually unapproachable without being seen. He would figure it all out when the time came. Right now, he had to concentrate on finding them.

He stayed close to the rock wall as he kept their trail in view. From a distance, there was no discernable movement, he blended into the background so well. His furs were almost the exact color of the rocks, and it was as if he were a part of the wall itself. He moved with the stealth of a puma. The muscles that had been stiff and sore from the gunshot wounds, were now supple, and flexed with every movement he made. His eyes were keen and conditioned to pick out even the slightest movement or irregularity in the landscape.

It was nearing sundown when his eyes picked out something that was not quite right up ahead. Immediately, he stopped in his tracks, letting his eyes scan the valley floor. There were trees off to the right about three hundred yards away, and to his left about five to six hundred yards, there was a group of boulders that had broken loose from the wall above and come to rest in close proximity to each other. It was here Dal focused his attention, because there seemed to be something amiss here.

He lowered his huge frame slowly to the ground, always making sure he was not silhouetted against the snow. From his position, he could observe his surroundings without any concern of being seen. After several moments, he picked out some movement from inside the protection of the boulders. He could make out three men moving around, and it appeared they were making camp. Two men left the camp, and went toward the trees in the distance, probably in search for firewood. From where Dal was, he could not see the horses for they were behind the boulders, but he did see one man bring what looked like saddles into the camp. Then he saw a fourth man bringing in the bridles

from the horses. So, they were all here. That was good!
Now he could deal with them on his own terms!

He decided he would backtrack a short way until
he was out of danger of being spotted. Then he would
slip over to the cover of the trees and make his way
to where the two men had disappeared. He had many
years of experience in stalking his enemies and had no
doubts about being able to dispatch these two without
arousing any suspicion in the camp.

After he was out of sight of the camp, he quickly
crossed the open ground to the cover of the trees. Here,
he could move more freely without any fear of being
detected. He estimated that he would have about a half
mile to cover before he would be close to where they
were collecting wood. The last hundred yards or so,
he would need to take his snowshoes off and proceed
as quietly as possible through the deep snow. Here in
the trees, the snow was not as deep as out in the open,
so he knew it would be possible. He silently wished he
had Molly's bow and arrows, for then he would not have
needed to get so close. He would need to get within
striking distance with his knife, and that was going to
be difficult.

After walking at a steady pace for several minutes,
Dal decided it was time to shed his snowshoes. He
would proceed from here with great caution, for he
knew that if he was seen, his mission would prove to

be much more difficult with all four men on alert. Right now, they thought he was dead, and that gave him the edge. He wanted to keep that edge, so after abandoning his snowshoes, he moved with great stealth from tree to tree. It was thick in some places which afforded him excellent cover, but in other places, the trees were sparse, with virtually no cover at all.

As he made his way ever closer to where he suspected the two men would be gathering firewood, he moved slower and with greater determination. Suddenly, from up ahead, he could hear the men talking and breaking wood so they could carry it back to their camp in their arms. This encouraged him because he knew they did not suspect any danger.

He continued to move in the direction of the sounds and was within about twenty-five yards of them when he first made visual contact. Their voices carried quite well in the still air, and he heard one telling the other about a woman and how familiar she was. He stopped in his tracks and listened more intently. This one continued to talk, telling the other about a time back in the settlements, and how the one they had just killed had saved this woman. It dawned on Dal with the shock of a musket ball, who they were talking about! They were talking about Molly and him! He had had no idea until this very moment, that Molly was the girl he had rescued from those other boys that day. How could it possibly be that she had ended up here in this vast wilderness with him? Why hadn't he recognized her? Probably because she had been just a scrawny little slip of a girl then. He himself, had changed drastically over the past few years. That was probably why she had not recognized him! He was totally unprepared for this new information! He couldn't even move; did not dare to move, for fear of failure, he was so shaken up by what he had just heard. He just sat there and watched as they filled their arms with wood and started back to the camp. He was too late! Now he could not make his move on them! He had wanted to catch them apart but now they were together and walking away from him!

Light was beginning to fade as the sun dropped below the horizon, and Dal decided he would now have to wait for the cover of night to make his move. Four men at once would prove to be, not impossible, but more difficult. He could not afford the luxury of a fire, so he settled down, resigned to the fact that he had four or five hours to wait before they would be asleep.

As his senses slowly returned, he concluded that Molly must be in their possession, which meant he would need to protect her at all cost. He would need a better plan now he knew she was in their camp. This he knew, he would have to wait for cover of darkness.

From where he was, he could not see the camp, which meant they could not see him either. He decided he would stay put where he was, eat whatever he had left in his backpack, and get what rest he could before beginning his stalk on the camp. He shrugged out of his backpack and opened it up to see what was left of the food Molly had packed for him. It seemed like it had been a lifetime ago when he had left Molly in the cave and gone off in search of these men. Had it really only been two days? No, he decided, it had been three. That first night after he had been shot, was just a blur. He found some pemmican, and a rock-hard biscuit. It wasn't much, but it was better than nothing!

He was about to start nibbling on the biscuit when his eye caught movement from the direction of the camp. He was surprised to see the two men returning! They had probably decided they needed more wood to make it through the night. What a stroke of good luck for Dal, and extremely bad luck for them!

Dal stashed his food in his pack and hunkered down to wait. He wasn't concerned about them seeing him because he was quite well hidden in a small patch of softwood trees. There was a blown down tree, and the root ball was a perfect place to hide behind. He watched as the same two men came back to the woods in search for firewood. They acted different this time, in that one would not talk to the other one. He seemed very angry at something, and Dal was pleased to see, that because of his anger, they kept a greater distance from each other as they gathered more wood.

Dal waited and observed as they drifted farther and farther apart. Slowly, he left the security of his hiding spot, and angled toward the man who was the closest to him. As he got closer, he pulled his knife from its sheath, and readied himself for the attack. The man was totally unaware that he was in any danger, and proceeded to go on about his business, breaking longer pieces of wood into shorter ones so he could take them back to his camp. Because of the noise he was making, he failed to hear any sound of an approaching enemy until it was too late.

Dal's knife struck fast and hard. The man was dead before he even hit the ground. Not a sound came from his lips. Dal quickly moved his body behind a mound of snow where it would not be easily seen from the direction where the other man was still working. Satisfied the body was hidden as best he could, Dal melted back to the cover of the trees once again, and then continued toward his next victim.

As he gained sight of him, Dal noticed his arms were almost full of wood. He knew he would have to strike fast before he headed back in search of his partner and then camp. Dal decided he would take this one on face to face and broke from the shelter of the trees at a dead run, his hand holding the knife high for the strike. He had covered half the distance between them before the man even saw him, but when he did, he dropped the armful of wood, his eyes bulging out of his head. It must be a ghost! This man is dead!

He turned to run, but never made it ten feet before he was hit so hard from behind, it threw him to the ground. Dal rolled him over and sat astride him, looking him straight in the eye.

"You dare come into my valley and wage war on me? You disrupt my life, and hold a defenseless woman hostage? You shoot me and leave me to die?", Dal shot question after question at him all the while holding the knife at his throat. "You mess with me or the one I love, and you don't live to see the sun come up!"

Once again, the knife struck, and Dal watched the light fade from the eyes of another one of his enemies. Two down, two to go!

Chapter Twenty-Three

Bill and Wayne had left camp after Wayne's little dispute with Jake to go fetch more wood for the night. Wayne wouldn't even talk to Bill as they got back to the trees, so Bill had gone off on his own to leave Wayne to wallow in his own self pity. Usually, if left to himself, Wayne got over his anger quickly and was his old self again. Bill hoped it would be so this time also. He hated it when there was tension in camp between two or more of them. He would see how Wayne acted after venting some of his anger on the firewood.

Wayne was fuming when he left the camp and wished Jake had left him alone to teach that woman who was boss. Sooner or later, he'd teach her! Nobody spit in his face and got away with it! Nobody! She would regret she had ever done that! He reached the tree line and started breaking wood to carry back to camp, not even noticing that Bill had gone off on his own, some distance away. So engrossed was he with what he was doing and thinking, he never heard danger approaching from behind. He had just straightened up with another piece of wood, when he felt a heavy blow to his back, and an intense pain shot to his brain before the spinal cord was severed, and his lifeless body slumped to the ground. He never saw his attacker.

Bill was lost in his own thoughts about how lucky they were that this woman had stumbled into them and given herself up. Tomorrow was promising to be a good day for them. They would follow her tracks and find the camp they had been looking for. Then they could live the rest of the winter on the supplies that were sure to be there, comfortable with a woman to cook their meals, and satisfy any other needs they might have! Then they could either head back to the higher country or go to the nearest town and live it up. Either way, it was gonna be better than the last few months had been! Maybe all this time he had spent in the mountains, half frozen, half starved to death, and all the time scared witless that his hair would be hanging from some Indian bucks' belt come springtime, was finally at an end!

Bill bent to pick up another piece of firewood and decided he had enough in his arms to take back to camp. With what Wayne was also getting, and what they had gathered before, should be enough to last them through the night. He turned to call out to Wayne, and what he saw curdled his blood! Coming straight at him on a dead run, was the man they had encountered years ago as boys, the same man they had just shot and left for dead! There was no way he could have survived those gunshot wounds! This had to be his ghost! Bill's eyes widened in terror, as he realized the intent of this man, or ghost, whatever it was! He was about to die unless he could outrun his pursuer.

He dropped his armful of wood and started to run, but starting from a standstill, he was at a disadvantage, considering his attacker was in full stride. He didn't go ten feet before he was slammed from behind and knocked to the ground. He felt huge hands rolling him over onto his back, and then this giant was sitting on his chest, with the very knife they had tossed into the bushes a couple of days before, pressed to his neck.

He heard the man speaking and asking him questions, but he was petrified, and couldn't focus on what was being said. He knew now that this was not a ghost! The look in this man's eyes was murderous, and he knew what was coming. He wouldn't have to worry about being cold, or hungry, or ....

One stroke of the razor-sharp knife across Bill's exposed throat, ended the thoughts forming in his brain, and his eyes glazed over as the life drained out of him.

Dal stood and thrust the knife into the snow to cleanse it of the blood, and then slid it back into its sheath on his belt. Now he had to decide what to do next. How would he approach the camp, without endangering Molly's life? He walked back to the tree line, and stepped inside, just out of sight. He didn't want to take any chances of being seen now by either of the other two men in the camp. As he contemplated his next move, a thought began to form in his mind. He needed to maintain the element of surprise, and yet he also needed to bring the fight closeup. Molly had been in that camp too long, and he was not going to wait until they were asleep to make his move.

Light was fading from the valley fast, and total darkness was just minutes away. Dal stepped out of the trees into the open where his two victims had been gathering firewood. He went to where Bill had dropped the wood and bent to pick it up. He filled his arms and turned toward the camp. He would leave his rifle here, but his pistol was tucked securely in his belt, and the knife was in its customary spot on his belt also. By the time he would reach the camp, it would be dark, which would make it hard if not impossible for anyone there to distinguish him from one of their dead partners.

He followed the path that Bill, and Wayne had made on their two trips back and forth. Soon, he could hear the sounds from the camp, but so far could not see any glow from a fire. That would work in his favor. If they couldn't see him, they wouldn't know him. They would think it was one of the others, and their suspicions would not be aroused.

He continued to follow the path, ever drawing closer to the sound of movement ahead. There was not much talking, but Dal could tell from the sounds that the two men were not close together. It sounded like one was trying to start a fire, and the other was doing something else. Dal knew he had to locate Molly fast, so he would know which way to direct the fight about to take place. The last thing he wanted right now was to have Molly injured or worse from a stray bullet. He took his pistol from his belt and held it under the bundle of wood, where he could bring it into action at the appropriate time.

He was just outside the circle of boulders when he stopped and listened more intently. He had been right about one of them trying to start a fire. He could see sparks flying from a flint as the man tried to light some tinder that apparently was not very dry. The man cursed as the tinder failed to light again and again. The other man was off to Dal's right and was apparently doing something in front of one of the boulders, about fifteen feet from his partner. Dal stood still, and let his eyes search the darkness for any sign of where Molly was being held. Suddenly the man to his right began talking, but it didn't appear that he was talking to the man who was busy trying to start the fire. Dal directed his attention to the sound of this man's voice, and heard him say, "tomorrow girly, you an' me are a gonna' git to know each other real good."

Then, a woman's voice, "in your dreams, you scum!"

Dal's heart leaped with joy to hear Molly's voice once more. Now he knew where she was and could carry out his plan. The fire was still not going, so Dal walked directly to where the man was kneeling and dropped his firewood on the other pile of wood that Bill and Wayne had already placed there. He turned and walked toward where the other man and Molly were. He needed to eliminate the one closest to Molly first, for he posed the greatest threat. As he turned to head in that direction, the kneeling man spoke to him.

"Is thet you Wayne?", he asked. Dal grunted and continued to walk toward Molly's location. "Whar's Bill? He git lost?" the kneeling man asked, without pausing his quest to light a fire.

Dal was almost to where Molly must be, when a spark caught in some dry tinder and sputtered to life. Slowly the glow grew in intensity, and the man added some of the dry wood, which started to burn almost immediately. Dal was now just past the point where Molly was seated on the ground, and as the fire grew, it cast a light on all inside the circle of boulders. The man closest to Molly, turned to speak to who he thought was Wayne, and the look of shock on his face almost made Dal laugh. Dal swung his pistol, and as the man came into his sights, just before he pulled the trigger, Dal spoke Molly's name so she would know he was there. Then his finger tightened on the trigger, and flames jumped from the end of the gun, as the bullet tore into the heart of John, and he fell at Molly's feet, dead.

Dal dropped the pistol, and grabbed his knife, as he sprinted toward the man at the fire, who had turned at the sound of the gunshot, and was now pulling his own knife ready to meet this unexpected foe. Dal covered the distance between them in two leaps, and they stood face to face, and toe to toe, waiting to see who would make the first move. Dal's face was clouded with anger, and he was determined this man would die. Jake's face showed surprise and yes, fear, as he stood facing this mountain of a man, who, he had been told, was dead. This was the first time Jake had ever seen the man they had been tracking and trying to kill, and he remembered the day they had first found the tracks of this giant. He wished now they had just let well enough alone! He knew he was outmatched, and he knew he was about to die. This man had brought the fight directly into their camp, and the outcome was obvious to Jake. They had lost!

Jake, however, was not a sniveling coward. He had years of experience as a mountain man and had fought in several knife fights. Up until now, he had always been the victor. He would not go out without a fight! Slowly, he began to circle to the left, always keeping his knife out in front of his body, and balancing on the balls of his feet, ready for any move from his opponent. The glow from the fire gave sufficient light for them to see each other, as they continued to circle to the left.

Molly had been totally surprised when she had heard Dal call her name just before the gun roared. Now she sat, bound hand and foot, in helpless silence as she watched the two men facing each other in a life-or-death fight. Only one would come out the winner, and she silently prayed it would be Dal. She hoped his recent wounds would not hinder his ability to move fast enough to avoid Jake's knife.

Jake's knife flashed in the firelight as he jabbed it at Dal's midsection. Dal instinctively jumped back, and the knife sliced air just inches from its intended target. Dal saw an opportunity, as Jake's arm swung past to put his own knife into action, and sliced downward, cutting through Jakes' fur coat, and into his forearm. The cut wasn't deep, but it nonetheless surprised Jake. He could feel blood beginning to run down his wrist. He ignored it, and swung the knife again, this time higher, intending to cut Dal's throat. Dal saw it coming, and pulled his head back, once again allowing the knife to pass harmlessly by. This time, Dal swung his arm in a circle, intending to distract Jake. It worked, and as Jake watched the knife, Dal swung his left arm, fist doubled, and connected with the side of Jake's head, sending him reeling backward, nearly losing his balance. Jake shook his head, and stepped forward once again, facing Dal head on.

They circled and circled, wary of each other, both looking for an opening, that would end this. Jake switched hands with his knife, and Dal could tell, this man was proficient with either hand in the art of knife fighting.

Jake faked a move to the right and parried a slash from Dal. Jake turned his knife as it slid past Dal's arm, and the blade sliced through Dal's fur coat, barely cutting his arm. The look on Jake's face displayed more confidence now, and Dal knew he had to end this as soon as possible. He still was weak from his wounds from a couple days ago, and any extended physical activity would sap his strength.

Dal followed Jake's example, and faked a move to the left, ready for the move he knew was sure to come from Jake. Dal purposely allowed his knife to travel further over his head on the way past Jake, knowing that Jake would take the opportunity to come at his midsection straight on. As Dal's arm extended over his head, he switched the position of the knife, so it was pointed downward, at the same time moving his body sharply to the left, which allowed Jake's knife to pass harmlessly by. Jake had been sure of himself as he had waited for just such an opportunity, and he had put his full weight behind this thrust. When the knife missed, Jake was thrown off balance, putting him at the mercy of Dal. Dal showed no mercy, just as he had expected none, and his knife struck downward, ending the life of one more enemy.

Dal stood for a moment catching his breath, almost spent from the exertion of the last days events. Turning, he strode to where Molly was still bound. He stooped, and once more cleansed his knife of the blood of the last intruder, before severing the rawhide that bound the woman he had come to love. Once free, Molly threw her arms around his neck, and burst into tears as all the pent up emotion of the last few days came to the surface. They slowly stood together, and she buried her face on his chest. Their arms encircled each other, and they stood locked in each other's embrace for several minutes before saying anything.

Dal put his hands on Molly's shoulders and gently pushed her back to arms' length. "Are you alright? Did they harm you in any way?"

"No, I'm O.K. You showed up just in time. They told me you were dead. Do you have any idea how that made me feel? I thought I'd lost you, Dal!"

"Well, I'm not real easy to kill! I know some people wouldn't agree, but I know God is the one who has protected me through all the dangers in these mountains, and He's the One who brought you all this way to me. You and me are meant to be together, and it'll take more'n a bunch of thieving scoundrels like these to keep us apart! Molly, I realized while we were apart these last few days, that I love you! I want to spend the rest of my life with you if you'll have me."

Molly wrapped her arms around Dal once again, and buried her face in his fur coat. The tears came freely, as she realized the impact of his words. He had just pledged his love to her!

"Oh, Dal! I love you too! I didn't know that I did until you left that morning. I felt like I had lost a part of me! Waiting for you to come back, was the hardest thing I've ever had to do. I don't ever want to be apart from you again! And then when they told me they had killed you, well, my whole reason for living was gone. I felt dead inside, just to think that I wouldn't see you again. You don't know how it made me feel when I heard you speak my name tonight! I thought my heart was going to burst! And then having to sit here and watch you fight, I felt so helpless!"

"Molly, I don't ever want to leave you again either. And I felt the same way when I knew they had you."

"Dal, do you remember helping a skinny little girl a few years back escape from three boys?", Molly asked, as she pulled back and looked him in the face.

"Yeah, I know, these are the same ones. They told me when they shot me, just before they left me to die. Molly, I swear I didn't know you were that girl until then.

210

I reckon I was too shy to look you in the face that day, so I never recognized you when we met out here. I guess love has a way of bringing people together," Dal smiled down at her. He pulled her to him again and as she tilted her face up to his, he kissed her full on the lips, shyly at first, then more forcefully.

After several moments, locked in each other's embrace, Molly said, "I didn't recognize you either, Dal. You're a little bigger now than you were then!"

He chuckled, and agreed with her, "yeah, I did kinda grow a little for a spell there. Molly, I'd like for you to marry me, if you would have me, and think you could put up with me. I know this ain't no kinda life for a woman, but I don't know no other way. I promise I'll do my best to make you happy."

Molly looked down at the ground, hardly believing what she had just heard. A smile played at the corners of her mouth, as she looked back up at Dal. "Yes, I'll marry you Dal. I don't think it will be too hard to put up with you, and as for this way of life, I absolutely love it out here. I wouldn't want to live anywhere else! And you've already made me the happiest woman in the world!"

Once again, their lips met and held for several moments. The fire in front of them was beginning to die down, and Dal said to Molly, "do you want to spend the rest of the night here, or head back to our place?"

"I don't want to spend another second here in this place. I want to get away from them as soon as I can," she said as she gestured toward the two dead men on the ground.

Dal nodded his head in understanding and agreement. "There should be some horses around here somewhere. I think we should take them with us to the head of the valley, where the grass grows the thickest. We can let them go there, and they can fend for themselves. They'll probably think they've died and gone to heaven! I've thought about trying to raise horses here in this valley, and this could be the start. There is plenty of grazing room and water here to support quite a herd. If we could get a good stallion, we could raise horses, and maybe even sell some. What do ya think?"

"Dal, I think that is an excellent idea!" exclaimed Molly. "I remember hearing the Indians talking about a wild stallion that lives higher up in the mountains during the summer months. They always talked with great respect for him because any efforts they put forth to capture him, always met with failure. Maybe we could get him!"

"Well, I sure would be willing to try, but our first order of business, as soon as Spring comes, and we can travel out of here, is to go back to the settlements and get married by a preacher! I'd like to go where my folks are for the wedding. I haven't seen them since I came up here. I reckon it's high time!"

"Spring can't get here fast enough to suit me," said Molly, as she smiled up at Dal. "Right now, let's get these horses saddled and get back to our camp. I'm hungry!"

"O.K., I have to go get my snowshoes and rifle. It won't take me very long. Why don't you put some wood on the fire, and bring the horses closer, so we can throw these saddles on them when I get back," Dal suggested.

"Don't be gone too long, or I'll leave without ya'," Molly teased.

Dal grabbed her, kissed her again, and then disappeared into the darkness. Molly threw some wood onto the coals, and in no time the area inside the boulders was bathed in light. She knew the horses wouldn't be too far away, and went to get them, taking the bridles with her.

She was right and found them all huddled together against the cold just outside the circle of light. She went to each one, speaking softly so as not to spook them, and one by one, slipped the bridles on. Taking the reins, she led them to where she could see to put the saddles on. Since Dal was not back, she decided to saddle them herself. It had been a while since she had saddled a horse, but she had no difficulties, and when Dal arrived back at the camp, she had them all ready to go.

Dal was quite surprised when he saw the four horses, and not a little impressed. Here was a woman not afraid to take hold and help! "Good job!" he said, nodding his head, as he collected the weapons scattered around the camp. Four rifles, four pistols, and four knives. He put the pistols and knives together into one pack and strapped it to one of the saddles. Taking some strips of rawhide he found in another pack, he bound the four rifles securely together, and tied them to another saddle.

"I'll put your snowshoes here on this saddle with the rifles, and you can ride one of the other two horses. I'm going to walk. It wouldn't be right asking one of these poor critters to carry my carcass around. It looks like they have had about all they could take," Dal said to Molly, as he went to retrieve her snowshoes standing off to one side of the camp.

"I'll be walking with you," stated Molly. "I don't need any special treatment!"

Dal smiled to himself as he took one final look around the camp. He hated to leave the bodies of these four men here, unburied, but he had no choice. Digging graves this time of year was impossible. These intruders didn't really deserve to be buried anyway. He did decide however, to move the bodies of these two, over against the wall of the valley. He didn't need to leave them scattered all over the place. He'd move the others at

214

a later date, if there was anything left of them. Nature had a way of getting rid of carcasses, be they animal or human. Sometimes, not even bones remained.

Molly watched as he moved the bodies and came back to where she and the horses waited. He took the reins of the lead horse and started up the trail without a word. They had tied the reins of an extra horse to each of the horses that Dal and Molly would lead, so Molly followed the second horse with her two horses in tow. It was totally dark as they started on their trek back up the valley to their camp, but the moon was just beginning to show its' smiling face over the rim of the valley wall. It was a full moon, and Molly and Dal watched as it shed its' light into the valley, illuminating it from one end to the other. They were each lost in their own thoughts about the events leading up to this moment, as they silently made their way back to the castle.

The moon had almost made its' entire trip across the sky when they approached the place they would call home together. The trip back had proved to be uneventful, which was good, considering all the events they had just gone through! Dal was still impressed how Molly could keep pace with him without any outward signs of fatigue. Most men would have found it impossible to do!

Dal, reaching the castle first, opened the door and went inside, with Molly following close behind. He noticed the firepit had wood in it ready to light a fire, just as he always did, and once again, he was impressed by this beautiful woman who was soon to be his wife. He got his flint and struck a spark into the dry tinder, and soon the fire was warming the inside of the castle. Dal went back outside and stripped the saddles and bridles off the horses and set them free to fend for themselves. He took the rifles, and the pack with the other weapons inside, and was met with the irresistible smell of roasting meat. Molly had placed that large elk roast back on the spit, and it was sizzling over the fire. The smell of the roasting meat set Dal's stomach to growling, and he suddenly realized how hungry he was! He took some water and washed his hands and face, enjoying the feel of the cold water as he splashed it over his face.

When the meat was cooked, Molly took her knife and sliced off generous portions for herself and Dal, and they ate them in silence, content to be safe in each other's company. After their meal was finished, they each were overcome with fatigue, and decided it was best if they got some much-needed sleep. Dal once again took his place on the floor, and Molly crawled into bed and covered up with the furs, enjoying the softness and warmth they gave her.

Just before they dropped off to sleep, Molly directed her voice to the corner where Dal lay, "soon, when we have taken our vows, we will sleep in this bed together!"

"I am looking forward to that!" exclaimed Dal, from his place on the floor. "I never was one to like sleeping on a rock floor!" he teased.

"Is that the only reason you want to marry me?" questioned Molly, a smile playing at the corners of her mouth. "'Cause if it is, I can let you have your bed back, and I can move on to somewhere else. I'm sure there are other trappers in these mountains who would appreciate me!"

Dal heard the humor in her voice, and said, "I reckon there are plenty of trappers who would like to have a slave like you in their camp, but none of them would probably put up with you for very long!"

"What do you mean by that, Dal Trent?" Molly asked.

"I'm only poking fun at you, Molly. I love you, and I can't wait until you're my wife. There is so much we can do together, and we'll never have to be lonely again. Now go to sleep, and we'll discuss this more in the morning."

Molly pulled the furs up under her chin, thinking how lucky she was to have a man like Dal. Here was a man who loved her, and would give his life for her if need be. She felt so unworthy of him! She spoke one last time into the darkness of the room. "Good night, Dal. I love you too."

Soon, they were both breathing heavily as sleep overcame them. The events of the last few days had exhausted them. Now, with all danger gone from the valley, they were free to carry on with their lives, to trap, and collect pelts to trade for next years' supplies. Most of all, they were free to enjoy each other's company.

Chapter Twenty-Four

Morning dawned bright and beautiful. The sun on the snow, was like diamonds, and as it rose on its' steady path, golden rays penetrated every nook and cranny in the valley. There was a definite feeling of Spring in the air. Warmth that had not been there just a few days ago, was now permeating the walls and floor of this spot that had been the home of Dal Trent for the past five winters. And now, once he and Molly could make the long trek back to the town where Dal's family lived, they could be married. Then this would be their home together.

Dal knew it would be a few weeks before they could make that trek, because of the snow piled high in some of the passes they would need to go through, but that was OK because he had a lot to do to make ready for that trip. He could still trap for a while longer. The pelts were still thick and prime, and he would need every one he could get to buy the necessary supplies for the next winter. Now there would be two to buy for instead of one, and he intended to look at horseflesh while he was there. With the five extra horses they now had, from the outlaws he had dispatched from the valley, all they needed was a good stallion, and maybe, if he was lucky, he could get another mare or two, as well. Two of the horses he now had were geldings, and three were mares, and although skinny now, Dal knew that as soon as the green grass of Spring started to grow, they would fill out into beautiful horses. He had always had a vision of someday seeing hundreds of horses in this valley, and now that dream was in reach. What made it even better, was the fact that Molly was now going to be a part of that dream too!

Dal stood outside the castle and let the sunshine wash over him, feeling the warmth seep into his very being. It penetrated into his muscles and made him feel good to be alive. Molly joined him, and she stretched her tired, aching muscles in the warm sun, as she spoke to Dal.

"I don't think I could have stayed tied up in that position much longer, Dal," she said. "My arms and legs were beginning to cramp, and it felt like the circulation had been cut off in my wrists. You showed up just in time, and I thank you for that."

Dal looked at her and grinned. "It was my pleasure to come to your assistance ma'am! It seems like I have been assigned to be your guardian! Of course, I would have gladly volunteered for the job anyway! I think the best course of action from now on, will be for me to keep you close by my side, so I can keep an eye on you!"

Molly sidled closer to him and swatted him on the shoulder. "Well maybe I should have some say in that!"

"Do you have a better idea?" Dal asked.

"I couldn't think of a better idea if I tried all day!" Molly answered.

Dal smiled down at Molly and wrapped his arm around her shoulders, pulling her even closer in a bear hug like grip. "I have to go out and check the trapline tomorrow. Do you want to come along?"

"I would love to go with you. I feel like we're safe now. I could really enjoy some time with you in this beautiful valley," said Molly. She turned her gaze up into Dal's eyes, and the look on her face made Dal's heart skip a beat. He bowed his head down and their lips met in a soft, tender kiss.

"I'll be leavin' about dawn. I want to get to each trap tomorrow, 'cause it's been a couple days since they were checked, what with all the commotion around here lately!"

They stood there in the open for quite a while, content to be next to each other, and enjoying the time together. The sun was at its' zenith when they became aware of how much time had slipped by. Dal was the first to make a move.

"We've got a lot of work to do before we can leave here tomorrow, so I guess we better get busy."

Molly agreed with him and went inside to tend to the chores there. Dal turned and went to his pile of wood to carry all he could inside for future use. It seemed good to him to be back in his regular routine. Nothing could compare to this life, he thought, as he loaded his arms with wood and transported it inside the castle where he dropped it on the ever-growing pile. One more armful would be all he would need, and then he could bring in some meat for their noon and evening meal. He went out and retrieved the final load of wood, and then went to the meat cache and brought in a choice cut of elk meat. He spitted it over the ever present fire, and leaned up against the wall and watched Molly as she busied herself with her work. She was straightening up the bed covers and getting everything in order for their trip tomorrow. They would need food for a couple days, a few extra pieces of clothing, powder and shot, and fire starter. All these things were handy, and it wasn't long before she had their packs secured for the journey in the morning.

The roast of elk was beginning to sizzle, and it gave off an irresistible aroma. Dal walked over to the firepit, and turned the roast to ensure it was cooked evenly. He turned and faced Molly and said with a smile on his face, "it won't be long before we can think of making the trip back to the settlements. Just as soon as the snow is down enough in the passes, we can go. I thought we could ride two of the horses, and take another one to use to pack our supplies back in. It's gonna take more than what I usually buy, seein' as though there's two of us."

"Maybe we should take two extra horses," Molly said thoughtfully. "I could think of a few extra things that we could get to make this place a little more livable."

"We can do that," said Dal, "but what we can buy is controlled by how much we get off our furs you know."

"Oh, I know that," Molly said. "We have some really nice furs, and what we get tomorrow will only enhance what we already have."

"Well, there is no doubt about it, this was a very good year for furs. They were really thick. They should bring a good price. I guess we should be able to buy a few extras. That is, if you behave yourself!"

Molly walked to the firepit and swatted Dal on the arm as she passed by him. She took the meat off the spit and cut off a generous amount for both her and Dal, and put it in two tin plates. She poured two cups of hot coffee and put it all on the table where they sat down for their lunch together. They bowed their heads, and Dal thanked God for what He had given them, and done for them. "Dear God, thank you for providing for us this food that we are about to eat. Thank you for protecting us from the evil that was in this valley. We could not survive without your help. We ask that you keep us safe as we check our traps tomorrow, and please provide us with enough furs to buy all we need for the coming winter. Thank you for bringing Molly to this valley. Amen."

Their eyes met for a moment, and they squeezed each other's hand, then silently ate their lunch. It was a late lunch, and so they would not need to eat much for the evening meal. They would have to be asleep early because they planned to be up before daybreak to get an early start. Tomorrow would be a busy day for both of them. The rest of the afternoon was spent doing little, but necessary things around the castle. Dal was outside, and Molly inside, each busy with work that needed doing. Dal molded more musket balls out of lead, sharpened his hatchet, and made sure his powder horn was full of dry powder. Molly spent time washing dishes, mending clothes, and sweeping the floors.

Soon, the sun dipped below the rim of the canyon, and shadows crept slowly up the valley until it was dark. Off in the distance, the moon was on the rise. It eventually would bathe the valley in silvery light as it made its' journey across the night sky. But Dal and Molly would not see the beauty of it this night. They were fast asleep in the castle, Molly on the bed, and Dal on the pallet of furs on the floor. Their breathing filled the castle with rhythmic sounds as they dreamed of their journey to the settlements, and a life together as man and wife.

Chapter Twenty-Five

The morning broke clear and cold with the normal silence of the pre-dawn. Dal was the first to stir from his furs and was placing wood on the still glowing coals as Molly woke from a deep, restful sleep. She swung her legs off the bed and threw a fur robe around her shoulders. "I left some of that roast out last night so we could have it for breakfast. I just need to heat it up."

"Sounds great," said Dal, as he filled the coffee pot and set it on the now blazing fire. "Coffee will be ready in a few minutes. I figure the sun will be up in about an hour. I think we can be on our way before that. Everything is ready to go. Our packs are full, and our snowshoes are out front. We just need to eat, grab our stuff, and head out."

Molly shot him a smile, and grabbed her bow and arrows from off a hook on the wall. "I can't forget to take these."

"You're right. Never can tell when we might need a little extra firepower!" Dal smiled back at her.

They both had a large chunk of meat they had fixed last night, with a cup of hot, strong coffee, and

226

were ready to begin their trek down the length of the canyon. Just as Dal had predicted, they were on the trail before the sun's rays broke over the rock walls to the East. They were content to walk in silence, enjoying the scenery around them. Soon they were closing in on the trapline that extended down the length of the entire valley. Memories of the last few days flooded in on them, but they both chose not to discuss anything about what had happened. This was behind them. They had done what needed to be done to survive. Life went on, and they had to live it to the best of their ability. And so, the events of the last few days, though fresh in their minds, and though probably would never be forgotten, would never be a topic of conversation between them. It was here and now, and though the present danger of intruding man was eradicated; their full attention was required for other things. Mother Nature could be just as deadly as any man. Probably more. And though Indians had not been seen in this valley since Dal had first come here, nothing said they wouldn't show up at any time.

As they neared the first trap, Dal slowed his pace to a slow walk. He approached the trap that had been set under the branches of a low spruce tree whose branches grew almost to the ground. Dal stopped about fifty yards from the set, and stood still, listening, and looking for any movement around the trap. Soon he saw movement, and as he trained his eyes on that movement, he recognized it to be a fox. He motioned for Molly to stay where she was, and to keep an eye on the surrounding landscape, as he made his way toward the trapped animal. He would dispatch the fox swiftly, and reset the trap. Then they would move on to the next trap further down the valley.

This was their course of action for the entire day, and soon night was upon them. They had taken many furs from the traps, even more than Dal could have hoped possible, and they were all prime furs that would bring a good price. They made camp under a rock overhang and soon a fire was blazing. Coffee was brewing and meat was cooking. Tomorrow would be a carbon copy of today, until all the traps were checked and reset. Then the whole process would begin again. Traps could not be allowed to go unchecked for more than one day. That would allow for unnecessary suffering for the animal, and Dal would not permit that. And so, the next month was spent in much the same way as these two days had been. Dal and Molly continued to enjoy each other's company, and grew even closer as time passed.

Soon the sun's warmth was melting the snow at a rapid pace, and bare ground was visible everywhere in the valley. Dal made one more trip down the valley to check his traps and pull them until next fall, when it would all begin again. His cache of furs was almost double that of previous years.

He and Molly were kept busy skinning, fleshing, and stretching the furs, and the pile had grown significantly over the last month. It was evident they would need two packhorses just to get the furs down to the settlements.

Dal stood beside Molly in front of the pile of furs. "Well, it looks like you're going to get your wish about taking two packhorses. We couldn't even begin to fit all these on just one horse!"

"Good, so maybe we should take three packhorses to bring back our supplies!" Molly said with a side-long glance.

"No, I think two will be plenty, but in the event we should need more, I planned on buying some horses, or at least a stallion. We can use him if we need to," said Dal.

"Speaking of horses, have you seen any of our horses lately?" asked Molly.

" Yeah, I saw them about halfway down the valley yesterday. They are making their way from bare patch to bare patch. I'm sure they are eating all they can find. They should be in pretty good shape when we leave. I oiled the saddles last week, so they're ready to go. We could leave anytime. I just want to give the snow enough time to melt in the passes, so we don't have a hard time getting through. We don't need to make it any harder on ourselves than necessary."

"Oh, Dal, I can't wait! It's been such a long time since I was in the settlements. I'm not sure I even remember how to act!"

Dal looked over at her standing there beside him. "You act just fine. Probably better than most down there. If anyone has a problem with how you act, just let me talk to 'em! I thought you liked it out here. You say you can't wait to get back there?"

"I only want to get back there so we can get married, and get back up here!" said Molly. She walked over and on tiptoes, swung her arms around Dal's neck. He reached down and placed his hands around her waist lifting her up until her face was even with his. He hungrily kissed her and placed her back on the ground.

"Oh, Molly, I can't wait for that either! When do you want to leave?"

"Tomorrow," was her reply.

"Well, I reckon we could gather up the horses today, and get our gear packed. We might be able to leave tomorrow or the day after. If we find too much snow in the passes, we can camp there until we can get through. The sun is really warm now and this snow can't last very long."

"Oh, Dal, let's do it. I'm willing to work half the night if it means us being able to leave tomorrow!"

"O.K., I'll go get the horses if you want to start packing up the supplies we'll need for the trip. It shouldn't take me more than four or five hours to get them back here. If you have most of the packing done when I get back, we can finish that up and leave first thing in the morning."

"Well, what are you waiting for?" Molly asked.

Dal stood there for a moment sort of confused with how fast this decision had been made. Then he kissed Molly and went to get halters and lead ropes. When he came back, Molly was already busy packing up supplies.

"I won't be any longer than I have to be. I'm hopin' they are willing to be caught. If not, it may take me longer than I anticipated. But at any length, I should be back before sundown." Dal moved to her side and caught her up in a bear hug that took her breath away. He kissed her and placed her carefully back on her feet. Before she could even react, he was on his way out of camp, with halters and lead ropes over his shoulder, rifle in his hand, and pack on his back.

She watched him go and then turned back to her packing. Soon she had all of the supplies they would need for the trip, packed, and tied together. She then turned her attention to the furs and packed them as tightly as possible into four bales that weighed about one hundred pounds each. These would be tied onto the horses, two to each horse, along with the other supplies.

She had learned all this from the Indians she had been forced to live with. Now she was glad for the teachings she had been forced to endure from those who had been her captors. At the time, it had been almost unbearable, but now these teachings served her well.

Down the valley, Dal was in pursuit of the horses that roamed freely. He didn't have a whole lot of experience with horses, but figured it wouldn't be too hard to catch them. He could see them not far ahead, as he slowly made his way toward them. Closer and closer he got until he was within earshot. He began talking to them as he crept closer. They were eating the new green grass that grew plentifully from the valley floor. As he got closer, they lifted their heads and looked at him, green grass hanging from their mouths, their jaws working as they chewed the tender shoots. Their ears were up, pointing in his direction, and they seemed genuinely interested in his approach. However, it seemed that the closer he should have been getting, with every step he took, they in turn, took a step away. The distance between them didn't seem to be dwindling!

When Dal realized what was happening, he knew this was not going to work! He had to come up with a plan! He tried to think of how he could entice them to come to him. Not having any grain was not a good thing. But wait! They didn't know he didn't have any grain! He carefully placed the halters and lead ropes on the ground, along with his rifle, and took off his backpack. He undid the top flap and held it out like what a grain bucket might look like. He bent down and picked up the halters and lead ropes to be ready in the unlikely event that they came to him! Gently he shook the pack and called to the horses. At first, they didn't pay any attention, but as he continued to coax them, they began to show interest in what might be in the pack being offered them. One horse in particular began to edge its' way closer to Dal, all the while nibbling grass as she came. Soon she was almost within his grasp. She stretched her neck toward the pack, trying to smell what was inside. Dal reached his hand out toward her with his palm facing up, and she placed her nose in his hand. She smelled his hand and then her tongue was lapping his hand as she tasted the salt. He was able to get one of the halters around her neck, and then a lead rope hitched to the halter. He secured the rope to a bush close by, and then proceeded to try his luck with another horse.

Eventually, it worked, and he was on his way back up the valley with four horses in tow. The three remaining horses followed along a short distance behind them. He made good time going back home, and soon he could see the towering rock formation that was over the castle. He never ceased to be amazed at how well hidden the castle was from prying eyes, even at close up distances. He and Molly could not ask for a better place to live. Everything they needed was within reach, and now they had each other, they couldn't ask for anything more!

As he drew closer to home, he could see Molly had been busy. The furs were all tied up tightly in four good sized bales, and more supplies were waiting to be strapped to the horses. Molly stood just outside the door and waved to him as he approached. He waved back and smiled to himself as he considered how lucky he was to have Molly in his life. He immediately chastised himself for thinking it had been luck, for he knew beyond a doubt that God was the one who had brought them together.

Molly moved toward Dal and took two of the lead ropes from him. She led the horses off to one side of where the supplies were waiting to be loaded and tied the ropes so there was no danger of the horses wandering off again. Dal did the same with the two he had, and the other three that had been following, stood still, and let them catch them and put halters on them also.

Dal went from horse to horse and inspected them from head to foot. He wanted to be sure they took the strongest ones on this trip. They had a long and tiring journey ahead of them. Molly watched from a distance and did not break the silence as Dal was busy with his inspection.

He finally had four horses picked out that he felt were the strongest and healthiest ones in the bunch. They really had done well to be in as fine a shape as they were, seeing as how they were near starvation when Dal and Molly had taken possession of them. That outlaw bunch had almost killed them. But they had been able to glean enough grass in the valley to gain strength and weight. From now on, they would only improve as the green grass would be thick and lush in the valley this Spring.

"I think these are our best bet for the trip," Dal said as he turned to Molly and handed her the lead ropes to the four horses. "We will need to keep them hitched for the night, so I don't have to catch them again in the morning. Can you find a place that they can find enough food for the night?"

"I already have a place in mind," said Molly, as she took the ropes and led the horses off a short distance from the entrance to the cave. She proceeded to make them secure where grass was plentiful enough to see them through the night. As she came back toward Dal, she said, "I'll water them right now, and they should be good until we head out in the morning. What about those other three?"

Dal turned and looked at the other three horses standing a few feet away. "I guess we'll take the halters off them and let them roam free. They probably won't go far from the other horses tonight. We'll just have to make sure they don't follow us out of the valley in the morning."

Dal walked over and inspected the supplies and bales of furs. "Good job packing, Molly. It looks like we are all ready to leave in the morning. I think we should be ready to leave at first light. I don't want to leave while it is still dark out, because it can be rather tricky getting out of here. No sense in taking any chances if we don't need to."

"I agree with you there," said Molly. "All I have to do in the morning, is fix breakfast, and make sure everything is put away inside. Then, as soon as we get the horses loaded, we can head out. Oh, Dal, I'm so excited!"

"Yeah, me too," said Dal, smiling at her. "You sure you still want to find a preacher when we get there?"

"You bet I do! You're going to be stuck with me whether you want it or not Dal Trent," teased Molly.

"Well, if I have to be stuck, there's nobody I'd rather be stuck with!" Dal replied.

Together, they turned, and arm in arm walked into the home they would be sharing together for the rest of their lives.

Chapter Twenty-Six

The night passed swiftly, and morning dawned with a cloudless sky. The sun was barely peeking over the valley wall when Dal and Molly came out of the castle with their packs, ready for their long trip down to the settlement. They were both filled with excitement as they worked at getting the horses ready. Dal took two horses at a time to drink from the water that flowed out of the castle. They drank deeply and when they were finished, Dal tied the bales of furs on their backs. Each bale had to be secured firmly so they wouldn't loosen and shift on the horse, or even worse fall off. Some of the trails they would be traversing would be on the side of mountains, with sheer drop-offs. If a bale came off at one of these points, it would be lost with no hope of recovery.

When Dal was satisfied he had done his best tying them on, he turned his attention to the supplies they would need along the way. When these were all packed on the horses, Dal turned to Molly. "I think we are ready to get going. Can you think of anything else we need to do before we go?"

"I packed all the supplies we will need, including extra clothes just in case. We have extra powder and shot, and I took all of my arrows. I think we are well prepared. You packed everything on the horses, so we should be ready to leave."

"OK, then. Let's do it," said Dal, grinning at her. He grabbed Molly around the waist and hoisted her up on the mare's back before she knew what was happening! Then, turning, he gathered up the two pack horses lead ropes and mounted his own horse. Together, they faced toward the spot in the valley where the trail would lead them up the shale slide to the plateau above.

Dal turned in the saddle and looked back toward the castle. They were leaving this valley, the place he had called home for quite some time. When they returned, they would be husband and wife. Together, they would face the future. They would return to Castle Valley and start their lives anew.

The End

9 781662 845574